END ZONE

The ball was snapped and Jimmy took it, clutching it tightly to avoid another fumble. He ran hard, parallel to the line, looking for a gap to appear. The other Porchester players threw themselves into blocking.

The gap was there! And Jimmy dived for it, head down. He was a scant yard short when the Castle Rock middle linebacker appeared, as though he'd been fired from a circus cannon, going helmet to helmet with Jimmy, who wasn't prepared for the violence of the hit.

His head snapped back and as he blacked out he felt the ball slip from his grasp. His last thought was a bitter regret that he'd lost it yet again.

Short seconds later he regained his senses and the first thing he saw was Hunter Goldblum leaping around in the end zone, waving the ball over his head.

Also available from Magnet Books,
by the same authors:

Laurence & Matthew James

END ZONE

★★★★★★★★★★★★★★★★★★★★★★★★

A Magnet Book

This one is for Bert Hewer, both as
thanks for all the work he's done for us
and also because he's a friend.

First published as a Magnet Original 1989
by Methuen Children's Books
A Division of OPG Services Ltd
Michelin House, 81 Fulham Road, London SW3 6RB
Copyright © 1989 Laurence James
Printed and bound in Great Britain
by Cox and Wyman Ltd, Reading

James, Laurence
End zone.
I. Title II. James, Matthew
823'.914[J]

ISBN 0 416 12202 7

1 'It's very deep,' said Jimmy Marvin.
'And it's pretty crisp,' added his older brother, Chris.

Their mother, Beth, laughed as she joined them at the window of their New England home. 'But it's not at all even. So much for good old King Wenceslas.'

It had been snowing again, for a whole week. Starting on January 1st, just after they'd finished their breakfast. Some days it only snowed in a casual half-hearted sort of way, as if the sky was almost hoping you wouldn't notice it. But a couple of times the leaden clouds had brushed the tops of the trees on the hills around, spilling their load of feathery white all over Vermont.

Many of the small country roads were closed, waiting for the huge, powerful snow-ploughs to come rumbling up to clear them. But the Interstate and the main highways were open, despite banks of white twenty feet high alongside them.

When they had the first serious falls of snow, in late October, Mum and the children had been amazed at how well everything functioned. Jimmy remembered Mum saying: 'Three inches in London and you'd

5

think the world had ended. Six inches and it would have ended!'

Now the teeth of winter were clenched tight on the throat of the countryside, the English family had come to adapt to it.

It was just over four months ago that they'd made the perilous leap, packing up everything and emigrating from Hither Green in South London, to North Strafford in the state of Vermont, halfway between New York and the Canadian border.

Burge Marvin, the father, had been born in America but had lived in England throughout his married life. He'd been a top-earning plumber until an accident robbed him of his health and career. Beth had worked as a teacher, but her money was barely enough to keep the family finances going. Daughter Kate was seventeen and had been working in a store in Lewisham. The middle child was an adopted son, Chris, who was fifteen now. Jimmy, the youngest, was thirteen.

Life hadn't been easy for the Marvins. During his childhood, Jimmy remembered moving from house to house. Each one seeming smaller and tattier than the one before. Dad had always been a brilliant cook, an interest he'd passed on to his youngest son, but he'd needed all his skill to make decent meals from penny-pinched food.

Salvation had come from the States.

Francis Marvin, the younger brother of Jimmy's father, had owned a successful gift and curio shop, called 'Bygones Are Bygones' in a hamlet called North Strafford in Vermont. He'd been able to buy a filthy and run-down café next door, and had offered Burge

6

the opportunity to come and run it as a quality restaurant specialising in classic English dishes.

All five of the family had talked long and hard about it. Finally agreeing that it might be their one and only chance of breaking the mould of poverty that constrained them all.

Like someone once said: 'If you don't have dreams, then they can't come true.'

So, The Olde Roaste Beefe had duly opened on time. And had been an instant success. Dad cooked and Mum ran the business side. Kate had found herself a good job in a bookstore in nearby Porchester, as well as a new boyfriend into the bargain.

Chris settled in at the Lynette Howell High School in Porchester, where his great height and strength had taken him straight into the gridiron football team as an outside linebacker. Following the steps of his hero, André Tippett of the New England Patriots.

Jimmy had always been painfully conscious of the fact that he was below average height for his age. Since he'd been twelve he'd started to measure himself against the edge of the bedroom door, charting his fractional progress. He continued this even after they moved to the white-frame Victorian house.

Christmas Day saw him scrape up to four-feet-ten-and-a-half inches.

But the last few months had taught him a vital lesson in living.

That it didn't actually matter, like he'd thought it did, how tall you were. He'd wanted desperately to become successful at American Football. His hero was Lionel 'Little Train' James, the running back for the

San Diego Chargers, who was only five-feet-six inches in height. Yet whose aggressively competitive rushing had made him one of the most respected players in the entire NFL.

Jimmy's nickname at the Thomas Melville Junior High School in Porchester, given him by the head coach, Christine O'Keefe, was 'The Pocket Thunderbolt'. A name that reflected his own powerful style of play on the field.

One of his great worries before they abandoned their seedy council house in Hither Green had been whether he'd be able to integrate in America. But he'd quickly found there was no need to worry. Not surprisingly there'd been a few bits of aggro. Some digs about his size, and about his ignorance of the peculiar differences between the English and American languages. He'd been ready for them calling lifts 'elevators' and pavements 'sidewalks', but he'd found himself getting very confused when he tried to book a return ticket on the bus. Eventually the driver told him, with the false patience of someone dealing with a half-wit, that what he wanted was a 'round-trip, kid'.

His skill at football helped enormously in easing him into the Junior High.

And brought him several new friends. All of them boys in his own class at school who played for the football team.

Best and closest was the skinny wide receiver, Hunter Goldblum, who lived in a village a couple of miles through the woods. The black quarterback, Eric Wood, who lived on the outskirts of Porchester was another good friend. As was the massively built Bret

Dillon, the tight end, who lived the other side of North Strafford and whose diminutive sister, Elena, was one of the waitresses at the Olde Roaste Beefe. The New England junior hurdles champion, Declan McMurdo, completed the quartet of boys that generally went around with the English teenager.

Chris and Jimmy picked up extra pocket money on evenings when they didn't have too much homework. Working as bus-boys, clearing tables, and as relief waiters in the restaurant. Both boys had felt nervous at first, knowing that they might finish up having to serve some of the boys and girls they knew from their schools.

Though it did sometimes happen, everyone up in Vermont was so friendly that there was never any kind of embarrassment for them.

Even during the times of particularly severe weather, the eatery flourished. They hardly every advertised, but they were rarely less than half full. Word of mouth spread the news of the great English cooking that was being served there. Tourists came, and skiers. And locals began to travel from thirty or forty miles around to sample Burge Marvin's menus.

When Jimmy wrote to a couple of casual friends back in Hither Green, he found it odd when he tried to describe the speciality dishes that brought the New Englanders crowding into the newly-decorated dining-room.

Rice pudding with treacle and raisins. Beef with onion sauce and sugared red cabbage. Grilled sole with mashed potatoes, garnished with parsley. Pork

9

chops with an apple sauce, roasted potatoes and minted peas. Steamed puddings that cut in thick, steaming suety slices, with delicious yellow custard poured over them. Haddock minced up into fresh-cooked omelettes, served with good old English chips. There were none of the American 'french fries' in Dad's kitchen.

It was only in the first weeks that Jimmy sent letters to the old country. Some replied and some didn't. But even the two or three that wrote back promptly seemed a million miles away from him. Homesickness didn't affect any of the Marvins.

Kate passed her driving test in November and bought herself a second-hand Renault to drive to work. The young man who ran Drama and Poetry in the Porchester book-store where she was employed, Deke Koslow, was becoming serious about their relationship, and seemed be calling for Katy most evenings. They'd go up to her bedroom and watch telly with the light off.

The American branch of the Marvin family were all doing well. Uncle Frank's curio shop had benefitted from the success of the restaurant and he'd taken on a part-time sales clerk. His wife, Laura, helped him with the business. Eddy was at High School, worried by low grades and a poor complexion. The latter was a more depressing problem than the former to him. His sister, Angelina, had dropped out of education and was currently devoting her time to a correspondence course in modelling. This involved her in a succession of faddish diets and hours of bizarre exercises every day.

Once they'd integrated themselves into their respective schools, both Chris and Jimmy found that they didn't really see too much of their cousins.

'Anyone fancy a walk?' asked Jimmy, turning away from the living-room window.

'Got to do some work on my history project,' said Chris, sadly.

Mum shook her head. 'Sorry, love. Too much to do around the house. If you wanted to make a few dollars more you could vacuum the landing and clean out the main bathroom?'

'No thanks, Mum.'

'Three dollars an hour?'

It was tempting. The record store in Porchester had a second-hand and discounted section and there was often something off the old Motown lists that Jimmy wanted. But that morning he felt he really needed to go out and walk a little. Get some fresh air and charge up his batteries.

'No. Really could do with a walk. I'll go up the blacktop and cut through along the ridge to the Sheridan Dam. Might see some mates there.'

'All right. Wrap up warm and don't step off the trail.'

It was a serious warning. As soon as the first snows came to North Strafford, Uncle Frank had called around and given the English Marvins a talk about the dangers of a New England winter.

'People die up here, guys,' he'd told them. 'Snow

comes sudden, riding the teeth of an old blue norther. You sometimes don't get a warning. Blizzard sweeps in from the Canadian border and it's here in an hour. Blue sky at noon and six feet before the sun goes down. You know what a white-out is? It's when the snow on the ground and the snow that's falling gets all mixed up and blurred, and you can't rightly tell where one ends and the other starts. You can be fifty feet from your front door and just give up. Lie down and fall asleep and never wake up.'

Eddy Marvin had told them ghoulish tales of folk vanishing in the winter and their bodies not being discovered until the spring thaw.

Jimmy realised that his uncle's warning hadn't been idle talk when he'd gone down to the store for some sugar. Snow had been falling hard. It was only about three hundred yards, all along a road, yet he'd very nearly got himself lost. Blinking in the shrieking wind and slipping over on rutted ice. His sense of direction had deserted him and his mind had trembled on the very brink of panic. The phrase 'white-out' came to him. Fortunately, the wind had eased and he'd seen that he was less than a dozen yards from the welcoming light in the store.

Jimmy hadn't forgotten that moment.

'I'll be careful, Mum,' he said. 'Be back in about an hour.'

Thermal vest and pants, with a thick plaid shirt and jumper on top of them. Heavy-duty jeans tucked into knee-high boots with a ridged sole. Then a scarf and a quilted anorak over the top of everything. Double-layer woollen gloves and a woollen cap completed his winter outfit.

In winter, the house was heated by its big wood-burning stove. A creation so voracious that they needed a pile of wood quite literally as large as the house to keep them going through the bitter months. Windows were double-glazed, and there was an insulated screen door inside both front and back entrances.

The boys had cleared a path to the garage and to the road, shovelling furiously in competition with each other. The metal blades striking sparks from the stone flags of the path, banking the snow up on either side. The wind cleared much of the corner where their house stood, but it piled up drifts across the main street of the village, twenty feet deep.

Jimmy's boot-heels crunched on the packed expanse of pure white. That was one of the biggest differences between the English winters he recalled and the winter here. When it snowed in London it seemed to be dirty the moment it landed. Turning to grey slush overnight. Here it fell in an immaculate, unsullied sheet, crinkling over the meadows and the rolling, tree-covered hills. Katy had said that it lay on the branches like snow in an early Disney film.

His breath plumed out ahead of him and he could taste the cold on his tongue and teeth. The air was like iced iron, bitter and sharp. He'd heard from his friends that it sometimes got so cold, at sixty below zero, that your spit would freeze in the air and tinkle on the ground. There'd also been some scary tales about accidents happening to unwary boys in toilets.

Dad and Uncle Frank had reassured him that most of the stories were exaggerated.

'Most of 'em,' Jimmy said to himself as he stomped along the ploughed centre of the back country road.

It was an idyllically beautiful day. The sky was untouched blue from east to west and the sun threw sharp-edged shadows across the snow. Jimmy ducked under the low branches as they dipped beneath the winter's weight, picking his way up the hill towards the old dam. From there in summer you could look clear down the valley between high banks, to a series of stone-fringed pools. Now, in the deep of January, it was a vista of white, with only the tips of the pines clear of the snow.

Jimmy paused, panting for breath, aware of the odd prickling feeling of the tiny hairs in his nostrils beginning to freeze. Despite the biting cold, he felt uplifted by the day. It was so bright and clear that it dazzled the eyes.

'Four months gone,' he muttered. Looking all around him at the white-muffled mountains that rolled away from him like the frozen breakers of some limitless ocean.

Jimmy thought about his gran, in her old red-brick terrace house a stone's throw from Hither Green railway station. Mum had been talking about trying to visit her during the summer. One of their best customers in the restaurant was a travel agent, and he'd promised to do them a discount fare if they wanted it. Dad and Katy wouldn't be able to go because of their work, but he and Chris had said they'd like to go back for a few days.

He stooped and tried to scoop up snow in his gloves to make a snowball. But it was too cold and it wouldn't stick together properly. Falling through his fingers like crumbling white sand.

Far away in the distance he could hear the yells and whooping of some boys near the frozen river. But from where he stood, perched on the rim of the giant earth dam, he couldn't see a single living soul in any direction. Jimmy shivered at the sudden feeling of isolation. Of being a tiny speck, balanced on the skin of the planet.

The thought made him feel cold and lonely and he shrugged his shoulders. He picked his way carefully down the bank of snow, to go and join his friends at their fun.

 'Purpose of visit?'

'To see my mother and sort out a few private details. That's all.'

The immigration officer at the airport had a thin, pinched face. His glasses were so heavily tinted that you couldn't see his eyes at all. While he was examining the passports of Beth Marvin and her two sons he was absently rubbing a small sore at the corner of his narrow lips.

'And these are your sons?'

'Yes. Christopher David Marvin and James William Marvin.'

Jimmy knew from the sharp edge that had crept into Mum's voice that she was getting fed up with the sneering official. The plane had landed twenty minutes early and all they wanted to do was get through the formalities and reach Gran's house. But this man was questioning them as though they were some sort of illegal immigrants.

'Your husband travels on an American passport? Why don't they have American nationality . . . Madam? If I may ask.'

'You may ask. That's your job. I imagine that's what you get paid for. Standing here and asking damn-fool questions so that everyone gets held up by them! I'm sure it's . . .'

'Mum,' whispered Chris, embarrassed by their mother's outburst.

'No need to adopt that tone, Madam. I'm sure you understand that . . .'

'I understand that you have a smart uniform and a row of pretty-coloured pens in your pocket. I also understand that I'm very tired and my sons are tired and I have a migraine coming on. If you can't stamp our passports or whatever it is you have to do, then kindly go and find someone who can.'

'Just doing my job, Madam . . . Really no need at all to . . .'

'Just obeying orders! Now, let me see. Where have I heard that excuse before?'

'Mum,' hissed Jimmy. 'Simmer down, Mum.'

'I will not.' Turning to the official, who was already handing her the three passports.

'Hope you enjoy your visit back home again, Madam,' he said.

'Home? Oh, yes, home. Thank you.'

They cleared Customs quickly through the green channel, though Jimmy had that funny feeling that they were going to stop him. Even though he had nothing at all to declare.

They caught a Tube train and found themselves coming into London in the middle of the morning rush-hour.

Jimmy stood by the doors, face pressed to the smudged windows, gazing out at the passing panorama of the summer city.

It was obvious that the August weather had been unusually warm. The grass in the parks and recreation grounds was a dull, dusty brown and the leaves on the plane trees looked shrivelled and lifeless. It had been hot when they left North Strafford, but it had been a gentler heat. The air moving between the hills, bringing a cooling breeze.

Dad had moved from cooking mainly warm dishes like chops and roasts. Concentrating instead on fresh salads. Burge would drive each morning, bright and early, to make sure he got his fruit and fish and vegetables from the markets. Having produce that was as fresh as tomorrow's sunrise made a lot of difference.

And the customers just kept on coming.

'Change here, boys.' Mum's voice broke into Jimmy's thoughts and he picked up one of the suitcases. Ready to make their way down to Charing Cross and take the Southern Region train to Hither Green.

Once they were southbound they found the journey easier. The morning rush-hour was staggering to its end and very few people were travelling away from London.

Jimmy sat by the window, his mind drifting back to all the years he'd lived in England. He made a conscious effort to decide what he missed and whether he was glad, on balance, that they'd moved to America.

'Penny for 'em, love?' said his mother.

'Just thinkin' it was funny to be coming back here. Seems we've been gone for years.'

Beth Marvin smiled fondly at her youngest child. 'Know what you mean. I felt like a real alien at the airport. And that rude . . . well! Least we've come to some good weather.'

The window in their part of the train wouldn't open and the carriage was stiflingly hot. There was a young vicar sitting nearly opposite them, reading a dog-eared copy of the *Church Times* and he smiled at the family.

'Pardon me, but I couldn't help overhearing. You're Americans, I take it? From the accent . . . certainly the young men?'

It had never occurred to Jimmy or Chris that they'd already picked up a strong accent from their time in the States. Partly as a defence mechanism to help them filter into their schools.

'Proper little Yankees, aren't they, Beth? Dunno why they gotta speak like that. Not ashamed of being English, are they?'

Gran was a lot ruder than the priest had been. He'd visited Florida to visit a cousin and was eager to talk about the country. But their grandmother was scathing about the way the boys spoke.

'All that sloppy drawlin' and saying "yeah" instead of "yes" and "sure" and all that Yank rubbish. Heard enough of that from them doughboy soldiers durin' the War, Beth. "Overpaid and over here," they used to say 'bout them.'

As soon as they decently could, Jimmy and Chris left their mother enjoying a cup of tea with Gran and made their escape out of doors.

'Which way?'

'School?'

'Park?'

Jimmy shook his head. 'No. Let's go an' see the old homestead?'

Chris looked at him and nodded. 'Yeah, bro. Why not?'

The red-eye overnight flight from Boston meant you often didn't get too much sleep. Jimmy had dozed while the film was on, and he thought he'd probably managed to snatch an hour or so's kip around dawn. But he felt really tired, finding the walk through the sun-bathed streets had an odd, dreamlike quality to it.

The exhaustion and tension that had coursed through his body when they'd first landed in the United States had been weird enough. But this was worse. When he talked to his brother his voice sounded to Jimmy as if it was being filtered between layers of cottonwool.

They eventually reached the edge of the sprawling council estate where the Marvins had lived for their last months in England. Since it was the school holidays the streets teemed with children – rattling past the two boys on roller-skates and bikes and soapbox buggies and glittering silver-flake skate-boards. Young mothers, heads tight together in private conversation, wheeled prams and push-chairs along the narrow pavements, wreathed in cigarette smoke. Several men were working on cars lining the streets, bonnets propped up. 'Hoods,' thought Jimmy, making the automatic translation to himself.

They turned left and then right and then right again, moving towards the busy railway line. Washing fluttered everywhere, taking advantage of the beautiful weather and the morning's breeze. A woman who'd been one of their next-door neighbours came towards them, pushing a clattering shopping trolley in front of her.

'Morning, Mrs Murphy,' said Chris, smiling at her.

'Who d'you think you're . . . ?' Peering through her spectacles. 'Oh, it's Colin Marvin, isn't it? And little Johnny as well. Thought you'd gone abroad or something. Or moved. Someone said 'bout the rent not . . . But that's just gossip, I expect.'

'I expect so,' agreed Jimmy, politely.

She smiled vaguely. 'Well, must get on, boys. Satan finds pleasure for hands of mischief. Or somethin' like that. Remember me to your Mum, won't you?'

They walked past her. A few more yards until they reached their old home. Chris and Jimmy leaned together on the front wall, by the squeaking gate. Each locked inside his own memories. Chris broke the silence between them.

'Doesn't look too big, does it?'

'I sort of expected it to be smaller than home is now. But its kind of gotten even smaller than I remembered. Funny that.'

Someone had moved in. There were orange curtains at the front bedroom. And the leaking gutter by the door had been fixed. A broken push-chair was in the front garden and the grass had been recently mowed to a crew-cut shortness.

As they looked at the house someone opened the front door and the edge of a face peeked out at them. And vanished again.

A moment later the door opened once more and a small brindled mongrel was pushed out. It sniffed at the door and then spotted the two boys on the side of the pavement. With a ferocity out of proportion to its size it came hurtling towards them, yapping in a high-pitched snarling tone. Jumping up at the wall, making them both take a few steps back from the garden.

'Friendly doggy, isn't he?' said Chris, grinning nervously.

'Surely is. Proper little Cujo. Hey, look at the time. Gran'll be dead cross if'n we turn up late for lunch. Let's go, bro.'

On the way into the heart of Hither Green the boys' thoughts turned to sport. Chris had been asked if he'd consider trying out for the regional team the next season. Jimmy's coach, Christine O'Keefe, had also asked him to try out at running back for his own age-group squad.

'And there's Halloween Bowl,' said Jimmy as they waited to cross a main road.

'October, isn't it? You had that rotten cold last year and couldn't play.'

Jimmy remembered the cold. His nose had been running so badly that he'd had to go everywhere with a box of Kleenex under his arm.

'It's the last day of October, Halloween. Day before All Saints' Day. The two best Junior High Schools in the area. Thomas Melville's only gotten through to the final once in the last fifteen years. But Coach says she reckons we got a chance. Here, there's a break in the traffic. Come on.'

As they darted over the road, an approaching car, a blue Cavalier, blew its horn at them. But they ignored it and pressed on to their grandmother's house.

When they turned into Leahurst Road, the blue saloon was parked outside Gran's home. And its driver was leaning against it, waiting for the two boys.

'Who's that?' asked Chris. The sun was shining down the street and it was hard to make out the silhouetted figure.

But Jimmy knew him. 'Jerry!' He shouted. 'Hey, Coach!'

Now well into his sixties, Jerry Meredith had once played pro football in the States and still sported a battered Philadelphia Eagles cap on his grizzled curls. He waved a hand at the boy who'd been his star running back in the Elmstead Victors gridiron team.

'How's the Mighty Acorn and his big brother?' he called.

'They nicknamed me the Pocket Thunderbolt over there, Coach,' replied Jimmy, proudly. 'And I'm not all that far off of five feet now.'

'And I'm fine too, Mr Meredith,' said Chris, shaking the old man's hand. 'Good to see you again. How're the Victors doin'?'

'Not bad, boys. How long you two over here in this green and pleasant land for?'

'Couple of weeks,' replied Jimmy.

'Well now,' said Coach Meredith. 'If you was to invite me into your gran's house for a cup of tea, we might . . . just might, have something to talk about. All right?'

* * *

His body clock thrown out of kilter by jet-lag, Jimmy found sleep difficult to achieve that first night in his gran's house. And the news from Jerry Meredith was exciting enough to make the problem even harder.

It was nearly two in the morning before he finally slept.

 'No, Gran. It's not soccer I'm goin' to play. It's American football. Remember?'

'Course I remember. It's the same team you used to play for, innit?'

'Yeah. Elmstead Victors. And Coach Meredith's got a running back off with an injured ankle. So he's asked me to turn out for them.'

Gran nodded, reaching in the pocket of her faded cardigan for a Fox's Glacier Mint. She unwrapped it and popped it in her mouth, flicking the blue and white paper at the waste basket at the side of the hearth. She missed, and left it lying there with several dozen of its fellows.

'And Chris is playin' too, is he?'

Jimmy shook his head. 'No, he's not, Gran.' Unable to keep the faint note of irritation out of his voice. Gran had already asked him that same question about six times in the last couple of hours.

'All right, all right. I heard you. No need to shout at me, son.'

Immediately he felt rotten for his lack of patience. He felt, rather than saw, his mother come into the room from the hall, behind him, and he turned. Seeing from the look on her face that all wasn't

25

entirely well. Without letting Gran see her, she beckoned for him to go out into the small kitchen with
her.

'What was all that about, Jim?' she asked, pushing
the door shut behind him.

'All what?'

'Come on. Don't muck me about. I'm not in the
mood for it.'

'You mean . . . me an' Gran?'

'Yes.'

'It's just . . . she keeps asking the same questions
and I get . . . you know.'

Beth Marvin shook her head. Sighing. 'Yes, love.
Yes, I do know. But you have to realise that Gran's
getting old. And when people get old they start to
have some problems with their memories. It's not that
she doesn't listen. It's that she really *can't* remember.
Not her fault.'

'She left a tap running in the bathroom yesterday,
Mum.'

'I know. And the house could do with a real good
clean from top to bottom. I'm hoping to have a go at
that tomorrow.'

'Me an' Chris can help.'

Mum smiled. 'That's a nice offer, Jimmy, and I'll
take you up on it. You have to go to training tomorrow
evening, don't you?'

'Yes. To try and mug up on the playbook again.
Ready for the game against Dave Sheppard and Wilburn and the Downham Destroyers. See if we can get
our revenge for last time.'

26

'All right. And try to keep your cool with Mum – with Gran. And tell Chris the same thing.'

'Will she get worse?'

They both heard Gran's voice, calling from the other room. 'Beth! Beth!'

'What is it, Mother?'

'Put the kettle on, there's a love, will you? I'm parched as the Sahara after a drought.'

'All right!' Dropping her voice to speak to Jimmy again. 'What'll happen? Don't know, love. Neighbours reckon her memory comes and goes a bit. It's a strain having us here and that makes her worse. Woman next door's got my address and she'll drop us a line if things seem worse. And I'm goin' to ring Gran up every week or so. Keep in touch.' She sighed again. 'Don't know what else to do. She'd never come out to Vermont at her age. Happier in her old home. Surrounded by all the things she knows and loves. For . . . for as long as possible. Best we can do, Jimmy. It's the best we can do.'

Neither of the brothers enjoyed being in England as much as they'd hoped.

Chris found many of his friends seemed uneasy with him. As if he'd changed in some mysterious way. Elements of the old, jokey relationships were still there, but they'd become overlaid with a strange cynicism that he didn't understand.

Jimmy listened as his older brother tried to explain it to him. 'It's like they think I'm a rich American. They don't see me as Chris Marvin any more. The

27

mate who lived in this council house by the railway line. Not any more.'

'I know what you mean, bro. Same with my friends. They're sort of uneasy with me. It's like *they* think that *I'm* goin' to be ashamed of *them*. That what you mean?'

'Right. Yeah, that's it, Jimmy. I was dead lookin' forward to seeing all the places we used to . . . sort of play and that. But it all seems smaller and not like . . . I'll be glad to get back . . . home, I suppose it is.'

'Only thing I'm looking forward to is the game against Dave and Wilburn and the Downham Destroyers. Apart from that, I reckon I would of gone back today. Or even yesterday.'

If Jimmy had known how the game was going to end up, he'd have been even more keen to get home to Vermont again.

'Good to meet you again, Jimmy,' said Dave Sheppard, shaking hands.

Wilburn Thomas was grinning just behind him. 'I'm even more glad your big brother's not in this one. Looks to me like Jimmy here's grown at least a quarter of an inch, don't you reckon, Dave?'

'Yeah. Must be all of four-feet-two by now.'

Jimmy took their ribbing with a good nature. 'Actually, I'm just about five feet tall now. So, I'm closing up fast.'

'Not fast enough,' said Dave.

★ ★ ★

28

The Destroyers, in their famous strip of maroon and silver, kicked off to the Victors in their newly bought uniform of blue and red.

Since it was a charity game, there was a good turn-out, as there'd been at the equivalent fixture a year earlier. When, the result had been a victory for the almost unbeatable team from north of the Thames by twenty-four points to seventeen.

Cornerback Tony Chapman caught it on the full and managed to run it all the way to his own forty-five, where his offense took over the ball. Coach Meredith called for a simple short pass for Jimmy to run a sweep play to the right. Quarterback Hebron Wayman handed it to Jimmy, who was ready to start a scything cut at the defense. The pass might have been good, but his team's blocking certainly wasn't. The Downham player, Mark McLeod, shrugged off a poor attempt at checking him and dived in at Jimmy. Hitting him hard around the knees before he'd even taken three running steps.

As Jimmy started to fall, McLeod grappled him, managing to strip the ball away, knocking it into the air. Hopelessly off balance from the force of the early tackle, Jimmy slithered helplessly onto his back.

The Destroyers' alert linebacker, Rufus Smith, was there, plucking the tumbling ball from the air before it reached the cropped, dry turf. Without a hand being laid on him, the tall Downham boy ran it into the Elmstead end zone for a first minute touchdown.

There was a shocked stillness at the sudden and unexpected turnover and score. Jimmy, picking himself up, heard his Gran's voice ring out in the silence.

29

'Is that a goal? Well, why did our Jim give him the bleedin' ball like that?'

But another voice came riding in over the top. Chris, shouting encouragement to his younger brother: 'Don't give it up, bro. Remember that it ain't over till it's over!'

The pumped-up defense from Downham didn't have very long to celebrate their startling early success. Tony Chapman made another excellent kick return, carrying the ball close to the halfway line.

Out came the big defenders, eager to try and repeat the stunning hit on the Elmstead star, the Pocket Thunderbolt, Jimmy Marvin.

This time around it was a very different story on the field.

On the first down the quarterback's pass to one of the receivers was ruled incomplete. But on the second down Jimmy took the hand-off and deliberately ran straight at the centre of the defensive line. Relying on his own power and determination to carry him through. Hands grabbed at his arm, his playing-shirt, his ankles, but he still burst down the middle, leaving defenders spread-eagled in his wake.

The Downham coach's son, Rafe Nickleby, the defensive back, was the last player in a position to tackle him. Jimmy feinted on his left foot as if he was going to try and dodge round him, then squared his shoulders and ran straight at the boy. Rafe was surprised by the switch, thrown off balance, and he clutched despairingly at Jimmy as he charged over the top of him.

30

The big crowd cheered as Jimmy coasted into the end zone, holding the ball aloft in his right hand, celebrating the score. The point after was good and after less than five minutes of the first quarter the scores were tied up at seven points each.

Jerry Meredith called his squad around him for a quick word before the special kicking team went back on the field.

'Great score, Jimmy. Makes me recall just how much we've missed that kind of aggressive, penetrating running. Well done, son. But just getting us into the game's not the point. They'll be watching extra hard for Jimmy next time around. What we have to do is try and tie up their quarterback-receiver relationship. Get in amongst them. Disrupt the pattern and don't give them time.'

On the field, everyone was getting ready for the kick off. Coach Meredith had one last word of warning. 'Remember, guys. Watch for Dave and Wilburn!'

One of Jimmy's teachers had once said something to him that had stuck in his memory. 'Talk's cheap, but the price of action is colossal.'

Despite all of the Elmstead coach's careful words and stern warnings, Dave Sheppard came on for the first down, just beyond his own twenty yard line. He rolled back with the ball from the snap, his actions uncannily reminiscent of the great Forty-Niners' quarterback, Joe Montana, and threw inch-perfect to his wide receiver, Wilburn Thomas.

The black teenager gathered the pass into his chest and set off on a jinking, dodging eighty yard run for the line. His offensive cover was all round, giving him blocks when he needed them, taking the defenders out of the game.

'Goodbye,' said Jerry Meredith, standing next to Jimmy Marvin.

He was right.

There were still eight minutes to go in the action-filled first quarter of the game and already the score stood at fourteen points to seven in favour of the visitors from north of the Thames.

'At this rate there'll be a hundred points up on the board by the fourth quarter,' said Andy Hopper, the Elmstead wide receiver.

The home team wasn't down and done for. The rest of the quarter was taken up by a solid, grinding offensive drive with Hebron picking up the safest options, using Jimmy on short yardage downs to eat up the distance.

Over seventy yards in an almost error-free push, though one attempted deep pass to Andy was nearly intercepted. Early in the second quarter the Victors had ground their way to the Destroyers' six yard line.

Coach Meredith called a time-out, beckoning Hebron and Jimmy to his side.

'They'll expect a short ball to you, Jimmy. Because of that, less'n I miss my guess, old Tom Nickleby there's goin' to expect me *not* to call it to you. I'm goin' to second-guess him. So, Hebron, you feint the ball to Jimmy, roll back like it's a corner pass to a receiver then Jimmy comes a second time. This time he takes the pass and puts his head down and goes for it. How's that sound?'

'Good, Coach,' said Hebron.

'Yeah,' agreed Jimmy.

Every now and again a carefully prepared plan will actually work like a dream.

The Downham coach figured that Jerry would call a pass play, rather than the obvious running hand-off to Number Twenty-Six, Jimmy Marvin. So he pulled away his defense, covering the receivers. Weakening the front line.

Hebron feinted brilliantly, then faked the pass. Jimmy powered his way forwards, brushing aside the first, half-hearted tackle. Tom Nickleby suddenly saw how he'd been fooled, yelling for them to try and cover Jimmy's storming run. But he was way, way too late to do any good.

The defense of the Downham side really tried. But Jimmy had the necessary impetus for a short yardage dash and he broke through them, emerging into the end zone with would-be tacklers draped all over him.

The rest of the half ran out in a defensive stalemate. During the break Tom Nickleby came around to where Jerry was talking tactics for the second half. He grinned and patted the older man on the back.

'You old rogue,' he said. 'Out-thunk me there, Jerry. Never thought you'd really call a running play to young Jimmy there. Good call.' Ruffling Jim's hair. 'And a fine game, young man. Well played. Let's hope the rest of the game's as exciting as the first two quarters.'

Sadly, it wasn't to be.

Very early in the third quarter, with Downham in possession deep in their own half of the field, Dave

Sheppard took a mis-timed snap from his centre. Unable to roll out of the pocket he was forced to retreat, desperately looking from side to side for a free receiver. But everyone had been covered by the Elmstead defense.

He started to duck away from an approaching tackler, but never saw the middle line-backer, Oliver Clark, rushing past his block on the blind side.

'Bad one,' said Jimmy to Hebron as they saw the crushing tackle. There was an audible crack of helmets and then Dave was thrown to the ground. It was a very hard but fair tackle that flattened the talented quarterback.

When the boy didn't move, Oliver himself waved frantically to the sidelines for assistance.

Tom Nickleby was beckoned on by the umpire. Jerry also ran on, offering help for the unconscious player. The crowd were shocked into silence as the huddle of grown-ups stooped over Dave. Wilburn Thomas joined them, shaking his head and walking slowly away, taking off his helmet.

'I didn't mean to do . . . you know,' muttered Oliver Clark. Jimmy patted him on the arm.

'Wasn't your fault, mate. Dave just never seen you coming at him. One of those things.'

There was a buzz of chatter and then a muted cheer as everyone saw Dave Sheppard on his feet. Leaning shakily on his coach's shoulder. The quarterback waved a hand to the crowd as he was led off the field. Jimmy noticed how pale Dave was, and that there was a thin worm of blood inching from the corner of his mouth. Jerry rejoined his squad.

'How is he, Coach?' asked Oliver.

The grey-haired American smiled. 'He'll be fine. Bang on the head. Don't think he'll be back this afternoon. Shame. Couldn't be helped. Both the boy and Tom Nickleby said to tell you that, Oliver.'

'Could I just go see him?' asked Jimmy.

'Sure. But come right on back.'

Leaving his helmet, Jimmy jogged around the pitch, joining the fringe of boys clustered around their coach and the injured Dave Sheppard. Who saw Jimmy and managed a sickly grin.

'Teach me keep my eyes open,' he said.

'You all right?'

'Sure, Jimmy. Right as rain. I'm the captain, you know?'

'What?'

Dave nodded. It was noticeable that his eyes weren't quite focussing properly and his voice was dull and level.

'Yeah. I'm the captain, all right. That's me. The captain. I *am* the captain, you know, Jimmy. Yes, that's dead right. Captain.'

Tom Nickleby got the injured boy to sit down. 'Concussion, Jim,' he said. 'Bang on the head. I'll get Wilburn's dad to drop him up at the hospital to check him out.'

'He'll be all right, though?'

The coach smiled. 'Course. Won't be on again today. And you're off to the States again, aren't you? Best say goodbye. Odds are you won't see each other again.'

The two boys shook hands.

35

Years later, when Jimmy Marvin was in a stand seat at one of the best ever Superbowls, he thought back to that moment. That handshake. As he witnessed Dave Sheppard being hailed by the crowd for his talents and being awarded the title of Most Valuable Player for the game.

Unfortunately, the concussion of their star player took all the heart out of the Downham Destroyers.

Turning the game into an ill-balanced showcase for Jimmy Marvin's considerable talents at American Football.

In the remaining minutes he ran through, over and around the visitors' defense for two more rushing touchdowns. Hebron also slung out a fast, low pass into the end zone, where Jimmy belied his lack of inches and outjumped everyone for the touchdown catch.

In addition he blocked all over the field on any play that didn't see the ball finish up in his hands. Twice on punt coverage he hit Wilburn Thomas with crushing tackles.

The Elmstead quarterback also scored with two touchdown passes to their big tight end, James Maddin. The Downham back-up quarterback did his best but he was leading a beaten and dispirited team. Even so he managed three touchdown passes, two of them to the indefatigable Wilburn.

The final score was a victory for the Elmstead team by forty-nine points to thirty-five.

* * *

Beth Marvin didn't talk to her younger son about the game until they were on the plane back to Boston a few days later. Chris had fallen asleep and the movie was flickering along in the background. Apart from registering the fact that Sean Connery was in it, Jimmy hadn't been watching it.

'Good to win like that against the Downford boys, wasn't it, Jim?'

'Downham, Mum. Not Downford. Yeah, I guess so. But after Dave Sheppard went off injured, they sort of fell apart. Jerry Meredith talked with me after the game. Said that winning counted for a lot. But it wasn't all. We didn't truly deserve to win. So, it didn't seem like a victory. More like a big kind of disappointment.'

'That how you feel, son? About the game?'

'And about goin' back to England and seein' . . . everything.'

His mother nodded. 'Know what you mean. Didn't turn out quite like I'd. . . . Anyway, we're going home again, Jimmy. Is that good news, or is that good news?'

He smiled at her in the dim light of the aircraft cabin. 'Home, Mum? That's real good news.'

 'Quieten down class. I've given some thought to today's writing assignment. Last semester we were discussing concepts of war around the world. So, I want fifty minutes worth of careful, considered writing on the following title. I'll put it up on the board for you all to see. And. . . . What is it, Molly? For sure. But next time try to remember to get all that done during recess. Before you come into my class. Good. Here's the title for your essay.'

Out of the window of the classroom at the Thomas Melville Junior High, Jimmy looked across the suburbs of Porchester, towards the rolling hills in the immediate background. It was the third week in September and the fabled New England autumn weather was already beginning. Bright sunshine with cold mornings and colder late afternoons and evenings. The leaves on the trees were starting to change colour with the fiery brightness of impending death. The greens disappearing and the orange, yellow and red replacing them. In another couple of weeks the display would be at its best and the region would fill again with the last surge of tourists. The Marvin restaurant, The Olde Roaste Beefe, would have a rush of even busier business. Then there'd be the only quiet time of the year, before the first snows fell and the skiers began to arrive in bright-sweatered droves.

'The board's over this end of the room, Jimmy,' reminded the teacher, Miss Abercrombie.

'Sorry, Ma'am.'

He read the subject for the essay, written in the teacher's neat, rounded hand.

'Bob Dylan said that Peace is simply the brief moment while the rifles are being reloaded. Discuss this point of view.'

Jimmy sighed and picked up his pen.

He saw his school-work as a necessary evil. Something that had to be gotten through so that he could be out on the school football field for practise games. The Halloween Bowl was looming suddenly closer and it looked like his school was in there with a real chance of getting through to the big match.

Generally his grades had been acceptable. At a parents' evening his teachers had all said more or less the same thing. That Jimmy was bright enough but he tended to let his concentration slide away at important moments in class. And some of his assignments for work at home had been hurried and second-rate.

'Good enough is *not* good enough at this school,' had been the comment that had stuck in the memories of both his parents. Coming from his class teacher, Emma Deurson.

'She warned us that any slippage in grades or behaviour could mean a ban on the sports, son,' his father told him. 'And I guess you gotta realise that your Mom an' me won't wait for the school to gate you from the gridiron sessions. We'll do it first.'

'A jolly good morning to one and all. Miss Deurson has already told you that I'm here for a single term on an exchange from a school in England. What we call a private school and you call a public school. Wait a jiffy. Think I might have got that wrong. Anyway, my name is Anthony Charles Eatham. Eat as in tuck into the grub and ham as in a slice of bacon. Easy name to remember, isn't it?'

The class sat in a stunned, shell-shocked silence, listening to the braying, upper-class English accent of their new teacher.

Mr Eatham had been expected for some weeks, but nobody had expected him to be anything like this. It was clear that even Miss Deurson found him difficult to understand and she kept turning away to look out of the window, barely muffling a smile, as he introduced himself.

He had breezed in ahead of her, with a broad and toothy smile pasted all over the well-shaved and perfumed cheeks. He was very tall, around six-foot-three, in a dark blue suit with needle-narrow stripes of light grey. Thomas Melville was fairly informal, but Eatham was wearing a striped shirt with a white collar and colourful silk tie.

Jimmy noticed straight off what a small mouth the teacher had, like a little cupid's bow, pursed in what looked like permanent disapproval. His nose was fleshy and tilted back, as though he'd just encountered an unpleasant smell. And the eyes were narrow and puffy. Though Anthony C. Eatham was only in his early thirties he looked sulkily middle-aged. At recess Hunter suggested, and they all agreed, that he'd probably been born looking middle-aged.

Mr Eatham and Jimmy Marvin didn't exactly hit it off very well, right from the start of the first lesson.

The subject was English, and the exchange teacher jumped right in with both feet. 'English, boys and girls,' he said. 'English is the greatest language in the history of the world, and it comes from the greatest country in the world.' He'd obviously been briefed. His eyes caught Jimmy Marvin's. 'As I think my young chum would agree. Wouldn't you, James?'

'Wouldn't I what, Sir?'

The jolly banter slipped a moment and there was a new, hard edge to the voice. 'Wouldn't you agree about England being the greatest country in the world? I mean, we English chaps must stick together when we're living in a foreign country. What?'

Jimmy was genuinely puzzled. As well as being extremely embarrassed. In the seat behind him he could just catch the sniggering of Bobby Sheldon. 'Cheerio chaps, what, what, what!' mocking the teacher's 'posh' accent.

'Foreign country?'

'Yes.' Snapped like a steel trap. 'America. Foreign country to thee and me, James.'

'It's Jimmy, not James, Sir. And this isn't a foreign country.'

'Thought you came from England, young man?'

'Yeah.'

'The word is "yes". Don't be so sloppy. Bad habits you've already got from your Yank chums.'

'Yank!' exploded Eric Wood, in the back row of the class.

'Who said that?' barked Eatham. 'I heard someone call . . . some undisciplined little lout. I won't have that sort of behaviour. Is that clear?' He paused, meeting only stillness. 'I asked a question and I anticipate receiving a reply. Is . . . that . . . clear?'

There was a mutter of agreement from the class. The Englishman nodded slowly. 'Better. I return to you, James. I do apologise; Jimmy, I mean. I believe that we'd reached agreement that you come from England. Correct?'

'I *came* from England.'

'Sir.' Prompting.

'From England, Sir.'

'You mean that you no longer come from England? Is that it?'

Jimmy was becoming more confused, aware that he was beginning to blush. 'Don't know, Sir,' he muttered, head down.

'Don't mumble. And stop turning crimson. Even a child of your age should be able to show self-control. Understand?'

'Leave him alone, you creep,' came a voice from the side of the room. Everyone except the new teacher recognised the distinctive tone of Hunter Goldblum, Jimmy's skinny friend.

'Right. That does it. That's it. Just because I'm new and a foreigner and a teacher and . . .'

'A creep,' interrupted a girl from the other side of the room.

The whole class erupted into a burst of nervous laughter.

But the joke became sour and flat when Mr Eatham kept them all in for the lunch recess. And every lunch-break for the whole week.

Jimmy and Hunter were walking near the staff-room on the Wednesday morning when they over-heard a hissed argument between the Englishman and their own form teacher, Miss Deurson.

'But not *every* day?'

'Perhaps we have higher standards of behaviour in England, Miss Deurson. And we also expect fellow members of staff to keep their nose out of colleagues' business. We support each other, my dear.'

'A teacher right or wrong! And please don't patron-ise me by calling me . . .' Suddenly spotting Hunter and Jimmy lingering in the corridor. 'And you two better get moving before I think about some extra projects.'

So they didn't get to hear the end of the teachers' argument.

Fortunately the class only encountered Anthony C. Eatham for four lessons each week. One double on a Friday and two singles on Monday and Tuesday. But each time was torture for Jimmy. It seemed as though the Englishman felt that the boy had betrayed him at their first meeting by not taking his side. He didn't

43

allow any opportunity to slip by without picking on Jimmy until he began to dread those four lessons.

Miss Deurson had also announced that Mr Eatham would be joining them for their fall trip. To an old harbour with sailing and whaling ships, called Mystic Seaport.

The visit was due in ten days time. Her news was greeted with a great wave of apathy from the class. For a moment it seemed as if she'd say something to console them, but she bit her lip and left it at that.

Eatham couldn't resist sticking his nose in where it wasn't wanted. He even tried to interfere at one afternoon's football training session.

The tall Englishman perched himself on the side line like an inquisitive and elegant vulture, watching Jimmy and the rest of the squad working out under their tough coach, Christine O'Keefe.

'Don't slouch, Marvin!' he called out. 'And keep your hands out of your pockets!'

'Hang on, guys,' said the Coach. 'Jog around while I have me a word with Mr Chinless Wonder over there. Whoops! Shouldn't have said that about a fellow member of the teaching faculty. But loyalty can only stretch so far.'

She was only a little below Mr Eatham in height and the boys watched as she stalked across to him, waving an angry finger in his face. He went pale, then flushed, spinning on his heel, and walked quickly away towards the main buildings of the school. Christine O'Keefe returned to her squad to a round of cautiously muted cheers.

44

'Boy, what an . . .' she began. Checking herself, just in time.

'What did you say, Coach?' risked Jimmy.

'Don't ask, son. Just don't ask!' Grinning broadly. 'But, since you asked, I pointed out that it was cold. That you were a running back . . . and a good one . . . who needed to keep his fingers supple and warm. And that you were under orders from me to keep them in your pockets. He mumbled something and called me his dear and vanished. Now, guys. . . . Not all that long to Halloween Bowl. So, let's play some ball.'

Hunter Goldblum's father had a weekend job a few miles away from Porchester, near the foot of one of New Hampshire's most beautiful mountains. It wasn't that Mount Cardigan was that high, but the slopes were criss-crossed with woodland trails and slender streams.

Hunter asked Jimmy, Eric and Bret Dillon if they wanted to all hitch a lift up with his dad and use some time in training around the tracks on the mountain.

When it came to the boring routines of exercises and wind-sprint repetitions, nobody was more enthusiastic than Jimmy Marvin. Much as he hated the remorseless grind of pushing himself to the edge of exhaustion, he still relished his own growing fitness. He could now run and keep on running throughout a Junior High game without feeling that his legs had strangely turned into pieces of cold spaghetti. Also, his power and speed over a forty yard sprint had increased enormously and he was in the top three on the squad.

So the following Saturday, having promised his parents that he'd finish his chores on Sunday, Jimmy joined his three friends for a day of working-out on Mount Cardigan.

All four boys had done themselves a packed meal of sandwiches with a plastic bottle of orange juice to keep them going. Hunter had peanut butter. Eric had a sticky chocolate sauce dotted with raisins. Bret Dillon had a lunch-box the size of a small suitcase that was jammed with a dozen sandwiches, all filled to overflowing with tomato ketchup. It was better not to sit too close to Bret while he was dining unless you wanted to look like an actor in a horror movie.

'That's really gross, man,' said Jimmy, shaking his head at the sight of the large tight end with ketchup brimming from both sides of his mouth at once.

'I'm a growin' boy, Jimbo. Anyways, what you done yourself to eat? Bet it's somethin' real fancy, ain't it?'

It passed through the mind of the English boy that he wished he'd done peanut butter. But he instantly cancelled that. He liked nice food and he'd inherited his father's interest in it. Why should he be bothered by that?

'Shrimp with sliced egg and a kind of avocado paste,' he said, 'with lettuce and tomato on rye.'

His announcement was greeted with a stunned disbelief by the trio of friends. In the silence Jimmy was aware of the sighing of the autumn breeze through

46

the top branches of the trees all around them. Of the tinkling sound of the nearby stream over rounded, moss-covered stones. A jay, scarlet-breasted, perched on a broken branch a few yards away, head on one side.

Hunter Goldblum broke the stillness. 'You made them sandwiches yourself?'

'Sure.'

The boy sniffed, looking down at his own hunks of bread and peanut butter. 'Wanna swap, Jimmy?'

The burst of explosive laughter from all four companions startled the jay into noisy flight.

The top of the mountain was a rounded dome of mainly bare rock, with an angular watch tower perched on it. There were already flurries of snow in some of the sheltered corners and crevices of the worn stone.

They trained by jogging along the trails, taking care not to turn an ankle on loose pebbles. Then they'd sit around and talk. The loose, easy talk that never seems quite the same when you're grown-up.

'One more run to the top and back?' suggested Jimmy. 'Time before your old man picks us up?'

Hunter shook his head, backed up by the other local boys. 'Late afternoon in the fall, Jimmy. Temperature drops like a stone down a well. You get ice once the sun's gone.'

'That's right,' agreed Bret. 'Mountain trails can be seriously lethal, Jimmy. Best just go home. Come again another day.'

 There were three coaches for the school trip to Mystic Seaport. Jimmy and most of his friends commandeered the back seats in the leading coach, spreading themselves and beginning to unpack their lunches. By the time they'd gone the first ten miles, they'd managed to eat virtually all the food so lovingly prepared and designed to last them the whole day.

There were six teachers along for the day and they'd been split up with small groups of around fifteen children. To the disgust of Jimmy and his mates they'd drawn the short straw. The teacher appointed to take charge of their group was Anthony Charles Eatham. Whose nickname was 'The Rotter'. A name that Declan had remembered from an old English public school story that his father had read.

The day before the visit, when they knew that they'd got Eatham in charge, Miss Deurson had called Jimmy and his group together.

'It would be quite wrong of me to criticise a colleague. Particularly one who is with us from a foreign country for just one semester. I heard the moaning from you guys, and I guess I do have just a little sympathy with you. But Mr Eatham is our guest and you make allowances for guests.'

Bobby Sheldon stuck up a hand. 'But guests didn't oughter behave bad, Miss Deurson.'

'Perhaps they didn't . . . shouldn't, Bobby. But that isn't why I'm talking to you like this. I think that Mr Eatham might be on the look-out for bad behaviour. For all of our sakes, take extra care not to give him any excuse to jump on you. Jimmy, you're probably the one most at risk.'

'Me, Ma'am?'

She smiled. 'Great face of innocence, boy. Yes, you, Jimmy. I guess it's because he figures you should be a buddy, coming from England and all. So, don't give him any excuse at all. Or it could be goodbye to the Halloween Bowl for James Marvin. And that could mean goodbye to the Halloween Bowl for the Thomas Melville Junior High for another few years.'

In the car-park the children were split up into their respective groups. Mr Eatham made a big display of clapping his hands to gather his dozen boys and girls around him.

'Quickly, quickly, kiddies. That's it. Don't dawdle, Jimmy.'

In fact, Jimmy had been the second one to the teacher's side, but he remembered Miss Deurson's words and bit his lip. 'Sorry, Sir,' he said, quietly.

'And don't mumble,' replied Eatham, tetchily.

Mystic is on the coast of Connecticut, to the south of New England.

It is a perfect re-creation of what a sailing port would have looked like in mid-Victorian times, with several different museums and exhibitions. As well as wonderfully preserved specimens of the old vessels themselves.

The school children had been working on a project about all aspects of whaling, including the harsh early days. Jimmy and many of the class were specially looking forward to going aboard the famous Charles W. Morgan, last of the Yankee whalers still afloat under sail.

At the entrance they had their wrists marked with a rubber stamp in the shape of a whale in case they wanted to go out and then return. Mr Eatham clucked and fluttered around them, barking out his instructions to keep them in order. He was so busy that he accidentally stepped on the toes of one of the Seaport's guides and nearly knocked him over.

'I'm really most awfully sorry,' he said, eyes darting around his group for a sign that anyone might be going to smile.

'Don't mention it, Sir. But we must urge caution around Mystic by all visitors. There is constantly different work going on along all of the wharves and quays. There are mooring-lines and other kinds of ropes around the place. An unwary step can easily lead to someone falling in the harbour. We would prefer it if that were not to happen.'

'Of course, of course, my good man,' snapped the teacher. 'I'm not the fool I look, you know. I mean, if I were half the fool that . . . Oh, never mind. Never mind!'

★   ★   ★

The grey water had a thin veil of mist layering across it, giving the old ships a ghostly appearance. The harbour itself was flat calm in the autumnal stillness, with a few fallen leaves dotting its surface. It was somehow the sort of place that encouraged quietness and the school party went about their business, sketching and making notes, without causing any trouble.

But Mr Eatham couldn't leave his group alone. 'Remember that you are not here for fun,' he hissed at Hunter. 'You are all here to work.'

'Yes, Sir. Right, Sir. Anything you say, Sir. Yeah.'

The Englishman peered at him, down his nose, trying to decide if the boy was sending him up. Finally shaking his head and striding away.

Jimmy called after him. 'Excuse me, Sir?'

'What?'

'Could we go on the whaler, Sir? On the Charles W. Morgan?'

'Yes, soon. Just be patient.'

'In her eighty years she earned close on two million dollars for her owners. Finally being retired in nineteen hundred and twenty-one.'

'How much is that in English money, my dear?'

The lady guide looked at Anthony Eatham for a long, long moment. 'Two million dollars in sterling? I guess that's around . . .'

Jimmy interrupted her. 'It's about one million, one hundred thousand pounds.'

'Thank you, son.'

'You're welcome, Ma'am.'

The woman looked at the teacher. 'I must compliment you on the excellent manners of these young people, Sir.'

Eatham was thrown off balance. 'What? Oh, yes. I mean, thank you very much, my dear.'

'But I'm not your dear, Sir, if you don't mind my saying so.'

Eatham flushed, his cheeks turning a darker shade of crimson as the boys and girls in his group burst out laughing.

From then on in, Jimmy and the others found it was like walking on egg-shells. Eatham was ready to fly into a tantrum at the slightest provocation. Or even without any provocation at all.

The day was wearing on. It had been announced that all the children would be allowed twenty minutes in the gift and souvenir shop, and Jimmy's group were due there by three o'clock. Bret Dillon drew the teacher's attention to the time.

'Five to three, Mr Eatham.'

'So?'

'Got to get to the gift shop.'

It was becoming colder and a fine drizzling rain had begun to fall. Mr Eatham wore thin-rimmed glasses when he was outside and they were coated up with moisture. The paths and walkways were already covered with a fine layer of glistening damp.

'Well. . . . Let's hurry then, children. Follow me. Quickly!'

The teacher led them along the wrong way, finding they were on a narrow wharf littered with ropes.

52

'There was a sign saying this bit was closed to the public,' said one of the girls in the group.

'Nonsense! Come on.'

Eatham bustled forward, picking his way along the quay. The others began to follow, huddling together as they tried to avoid slipping. A man appeared from the mist shouting at the party.

'Hey! Didn't you see the sign? You can't come along here. It's closed to the public. Go on back and be careful.'

'Frightfully sorry. Stupid boys and girls! Didn't any of you see the warning? Get back! Quickly! Get on back!'

The teacher started to push them around, jostling the ones nearest him, who in their turn knocked into others.

It all happened ridiculously quickly.

Bobby Sheldon was near the edge of the dock, ten feet above the chilly water of the harbour. Eric Wood was immediately in front of him. Jimmy was at the side, pressed against the wooden wall of one of the buildings, glancing towards Anthony Eatham.

Brimming with self-importance, the Englishman was looking towards the worker, still mouthing apologies. He tripped over a coil of rope.

Bobby Sheldon was pushed hard in the small of the back.

Taken by surprise, the boy also stumbled.

And pushed Eric Wood over the edge into the water.

★   ★   ★

It was a moment of frozen time. Like an insect trapped for ever in a bead of amber. The black teenager toppling sideways, mouth open in a yell of shock, arms flailing.

A huge fountain hanging in the air. The worker dived instantly off the quay and dragged the boy from the harbour. Eric shivered with cold, complaining that he'd banged his wrist on the edge of the wharf as he went in. There was a chaos of babble and screams, and Mr Eatham bellowed for calm.

Miss Deurson appeared from nowhere, taking immediate charge of the situation, calming the near panic amongst the group.

'I don't want to hold a post-mortem right here and now. That can wait. But while things are fresh in everyone's memory, mebbe we can just try and clarify what happened?'

There were Bobby Sheldon, Jimmy, two girls and one more boy, standing in a half-circle around Miss Deurson. Mr Eatham stood at her side, hands folded solemnly in front of himself.

The other boy and the girls all said they'd seen nothing. Bobby claimed he'd been pushed from behind and had gone into Eric.

'Not true,' said Eatham, piously. 'I'm sorry to say that Sheldon, in my clear sight, knocked into the black child and threw him into the harbour. I could do nothing to save him.'

'No,' said Bobby in a tiny, shocked voice. 'Not true, Ma'am.'

Jimmy didn't speak. They were in the car-park of

Mystic Seaport and the fog was swirling in off the sea. The coaches were all ready to go back to Porchester, their windows lined with interested faces, pressed against the glass.

Everything seemed perfectly normal. Yet the boy knew that he'd just heard his teacher tell an outrageous lie to try and shift blame on to an innocent person. Jimmy knew that. He'd *seen* what had actually happened to Eric Wood.

'True, I'm afraid. I trust the boy will be severely punished, Miss Deurson.'

'I didn't, Ma'am,' protested Bobby. 'Truly, I didn't.'

Miss Deurson half-turned to face Jimmy Marvin. Mr Eatham also stared at him, almost smiling in his triumph. 'Jimmy?' she said.

'Mr Eatham is lying, Ma'am. He tripped, pushed Bobby Sheldon and he knocked Eric into the harbour.'

All of a sudden, Jimmy desperately wanted to go to the toilet.

 'What did he say, bro?'

Chris had been out late to the movies and had come back to hear all about the dramatic events at Mystic Seaport. He'd bounded up the stairs, knocked and then gone into Jimmy's bedroom. To find his younger brother sitting on his bed, reading a book called *Rumblefish*.

'You mean when I said that he wasn't telling the truth?'

'Yeah.'

Jimmy thought back to that moment in the wreathing mist, and shivered like someone had just walked across his grave.

In the second or so after he'd spoken, he saw all the blood drain from the Englishman's face. The puffy eyes opened wide and the jaw dropped. For a moment his right hand started to lift, as if he was going to lash out and slap Jimmy across the face. Miss Deurson saw the movement and took a half-step forwards, putting herself between her colleague and the frightened boy.

'She said that it wasn't the time or place to sort things out. The coaches would be late getting back to school.'

'What did the Rotter say?'

56

'Nothin' much. Sort of glared, and muttered that she was probably right. But it wasn't goin' to end like that. Tried to make himself sound like Clint Eastwood.'

'What'll happen?'

Jimmy shook his head. 'Dunno, bro. Suppose Miss Deurson'll find out the truth. Somehow. I mean, he's a teacher. He can't just tell a lie and. . . . You know what I mean, Chris?'

'Sure, sure,' he replied, trying to sound reassuring.

The next day was one of those that Jimmy's class didn't have Mr Eatham for a lesson. But they did have Miss Deurson.

Their class teacher was late arriving and when she swept into the classroom she looked flustered, spots of crimson on her cheek-bones. She glanced towards Jimmy and then looked away again. Almost as though she was embarrassed.

'Sit quietly and find something to do. Some reading. I want Bobby Sheldon and Jimmy Marvin to come up here to my desk for a minute.'

The two boys exchanged glances as they picked their way to the front. There'd been some discussion about Eric Wood not being in school that morning.

Miss Deurson looked up at them, motioning them closer. Jimmy spoke first. 'Is Eric all right, Ma'am? Only he's not . . .'

'Badly bruised wrist. He'll be in on Monday.'

'Will he be fit for the Halloween Bowl?' asked Bobby Sheldon. 'Only he's really one of our key players. Him and Jimmy. Lose either and . . .'

57

'We are not here to discuss the prospects for the football squad, Robert! But I believe that Eric will be fit for the match.'

The two boys grinned at each other in relief.

But the teacher hadn't finished. 'Nothing to smile about, guys. Believe me. I've just come from a very heavy meet with the Principal and with Mr Eatham, and there is nothing to smile about.'

Once again, Jimmy had an uncomfortable feeling in his stomach. In his year at the Thomas Melville Junior High he'd never seen any of the teachers look as serious and gloomy as Miss Deurson.

'What happened, Ma'am?' asked Bobby Sheldon.

'Our English exchange colleague insists absolutely on standing by his story.'

'But it's not true,' said Jimmy.

She reached out a hand and gripped him by the sleeve. 'Listen to me, Jimmy, and listen to me very carefully. Nobody saw what happened except you. Bobby didn't actually see it. Mr Eatham makes that point very forcibly. And don't tell me you felt it, Bobby. That's not the point. It all comes down to something very simple.'

'Yeah,' said Jimmy. 'My word 'gainst his.'

The woman nodded. 'I realise that this is not easy for you. Mr Eatham is only here for another five weeks or so. The Principal, Doctor Montgomery, has darned little choice.'

'He believes Eatham,' sighed Jimmy.

Miss Deurson still had hold of his sleeve. 'He *has* to believe him, son. That isn't the same as saying that he

58

does believe him. You're old enough to realise there's a difference.'

'Sure. I'm tellin' the truth. Bobby knows it. I reckon you know it. And you say that Doc Montgomery knows it as well. I get the crap and Eatham comes out smelling of roses.'

She let him go. 'Don't use that kind of language in my class, Jimmy. I don't care how bitter you feel.'

'That's real unfair, Ma'am,' said Bobby in a sullen voice.

'Nobody ever said life was fair. Now Mr Eatham doesn't want you punished, Bobby. He says that . . . that he believes you are just mistaken.'

'What about me?'

She waved Bobby back to his place, waiting until he'd gone from earshot. 'I have asked that you should not be punished for what you said. But Mr Eatham feels you are a ringleader of the opposition to his teaching. Please don't say anything, there's a good boy, Jimmy. Now, he has said he'll think about it and talk to you later. I imagine it will be some extra work or possibly a detention or two. I hope that's all.'

Jimmy didn't finally see Anthony Eatham until the following afternoon, in the middle of the gridiron training session.

Eric had turned up for school with his wrist bandaged, nearly giving Coach O'Keefe a heart attack. But he'd reassured her that he would definitely be fit in time for the Halloween Bowl.

They now knew when the match was to be played and who their opponents would be. It was a Saturday afternoon game, at the main stadium in Porchester. As it happened, that actually was the right day for Halloween. The Thomas Melville boys would be matched against a team from about thirty miles north, called the Castle Rock Junior High. They'd won Halloween Bowl four times in the last five years and were strong favourites to triumph again this year.

Jimmy hadn't been able to find one of his socks and was late on to the field. He walked across with Eric, the two boys laughing in the autumnal sunshine. In Eric's place, Hunter Goldblum was playing as stand-by quarterback.

On the side of the practise pitch nearest to the school buildings their kicker was shooting field goals into a home-made net, patched together from a pair of blankets bound between two vertical posts. Jimmy laughed as one of the kicks caromed off the stretched material, making their kicker dive sideways to avoid being hit by the ball.

'Gets you ready for them chargin' it down!' yelled Eric, joining in Jimmy's laughter.

Andrew Poscotis, their punter, was near them, practising taking snaps of the ball, then booting it far down the field to the other kick return specialist on the squad. He would take a few jigging, feinting steps then throw the ball back to the centre for them to repeat the move.

Just to keep his own skills well honed, Jimmy jogged down and caught a few punts himself.

He noticed that Christine O'Keefe was working with the linebackers and he waved to her. She waved back, but he thought she was looking a bit worried.

Obviously because the Halloween Bowl was such a prestigious game and the pressure was getting to her.

Jeremiah Carson called to him from the sideline and Jimmy strolled over to speak to him. Though he was only the same age as Jimmy, he was the chief assistant coach for the defense. A snow-cat had overturned on him when he'd only been five years old, leaving him with a succession of operations and one leg three inches shorter than the other. But he had an incredibly keen football brain and pushed his enthusiasm into coaching.

'Hi, my man,' he said. 'Hear the Rotter's been giving you some aggravation.'

'Yeah. But it looks like it's all blown over. How's things with you?'

'Good. Gettin' the linemen here to batter the heck out of the tackle dummy. Nearly got it down and done for.'

Jimmy watched as the group of boys psyched themselves up for what they hoped to do to the Castle Rock quarterback in a couple of weeks. Leaping on the dummy and pounding it to the ground. Ripping at it until the stuffing of rags all spilled out. One of the biggest of the team held up the limp remains with a triumphant whoop of glee.

'How 'bout that, Jeremiah? We get to hang him up with the rest?'

'Sure thing, Moose. Take it away and ask Coach O'Keefe for a new tackling dummy.'

The dressing-room wall had a collage of the eviscerated shells of previous dummies. It all helped to boost everyone's enthusiasm for the big match.

'Better go and join my own unit, man,' said Jimmy, patting Jeremiah on the shoulder. 'Take care and have a nice day.'

Hunter and the rest of the offense were doing warming-up exercises for stretching and suppleness. Jimmy sat on the cool turf next to Declan McMurdo and began his own work-out.

While they worked and sweated, their coach took them again through the main offensive plays for the big game. Then they split up once more into smaller groups.

Linemen rehearsed blocking invisible defenders and the receivers tried to break clear of phantom defensive backs. Jimmy and Declan took short passes and sprinted at their ghostly opposite numbers.

'All right, guys! Gather round. I know we don't have Eric here to work-out for today, but I want us to practise that trick play called, "Three L Way Right". Everyone know it?' General nodding of heads from the squad. She looked around, her eyes settling on the punter. 'Andy, you tell us?'

'I won't be in the play, Coach,' he protested.

'You never know. A couple of injuries and. . . . I want everyone to know all the key plays.'

'I do know it, Coach.'

'Go on then. Three L Way Right.'

'Sure. Looks like a normal close hand-off to Jimmy. He starts to run, then cuts back in the opposite direction. While he's doing that the quarterback tries to scramble around to the right. If he gets clear then Jimmy suddenly passes to him.'

'Good, Andy. I'm pleased. So, let's try it out, guys.'

Hunter took Eric's place, while the black boy stood on the side, watching closely. As they lined up, Jimmy noticed a tall figure come out of the main school building and down the flight of wide stone steps, towards the playing-field. Even at that distance he couldn't mistake Anthony Eatham, Esquire. He wondered what the English teacher was doing. He'd not shown any previous interest in sport.

But the play was called and his mind clicked into total concentration.

'Three L Way Right,' shouted Hunter, crouched behind the centre for the snap. 'Hut, hut, hut.' The ball was in his fingers on the third count.

Jimmy was in for the pass, cradling it to his chest, faking the run. Watching as Hunter sneaked away round the end of the defensive line, who were focussing their energy on covering the running back.

'Now!' yelled the coach.

Jimmy planted his feet and changed direction, seeing Hunter in the clear, waving his arm for the pass. He cocked his wrist and heaved the ball, seeing it spin like a torpedo, landing in the arms of the substitute quarterback.

Who dropped it.

'Oh, shoot!' he yelled, punching his right fist into the palm of his left hand.

'Don't worry, son,' said Coach O'Keefe. 'I may call it in the Bowl. And I may not. What d'you reckon, Jimmy.'

'Didn't feel quite right, Coach. But it's partly not having Eric there. I'll get it right on the day. No problem.'

'I'm afraid that there is a touch of a problem, Master Marvin. Rather a serious problem, don't you know.'

Christine O'Keefe spun round to face the interruption. 'Mr Eatham. Do you mind? Jimmy is a key player in my plans for the Halloween Bowl.'

There was a hateful smug smile on the man's face. 'Really, my dear? Well you'd better change your plans. I've just persuaded Principal Montgomery to ban the young man from all games for two weeks.' He turned round to walk away, throwing over his shoulder. 'I'm frightfully sorry.'

 For the next few days Jimmy Marvin dragged around as though someone had filled his heart with cold lead.

School was wearisome and the English lessons almost intolerable. And when he came home to North Strafford he generally went up to his own bedroom and closed the door, lying on his bed for hours on end, staring at the ceiling.

Both Mum and Dad had tried to talk him out of the gloom. And both his parents had failed to cheer him up at all.

'It wouldn't be like this if I'd done something wrong. Anything wrong. But I'm tellin' the truth and the Rotter's tellin' lies. He walks round grinning like a cat who's got the salmon and I'm barred from gridiron. Not just me! It means we've all lost the Halloween Bowl game!'

At fourteen years of age, Jimmy hadn't cried for nearly three years. But twice during that week, in the small hours of the morning when the blood flows slowest, Chris, in the room next door, heard his younger brother sobbing his heart out.

It *was* all so unfair.

* * *

The English teacher's decision to ban Jimmy from playing gridiron caused so much trouble at the Thomas Melville Junior High that even Principal Montgomery became involved. Calling for Jimmy on the Thursday of the first week. Nine days from the big match.

The weather had become much colder and the northerly wind carried a few flakes of snow on its breath as it swirled around the classrooms. By late afternoon the temperature was often falling well below freezing.

Jimmy walked along the corridor, pushing open the door to the secretary's office. Miss Stubbs smiled at him. 'Principal's expecting you, Jimmy. Go right on in.'

'Come in. Sit down.' The head of the Junior High, Harold Montgomery, was a middle-aged man with a straggling ginger moustache. An accident had left him with the corner of his mouth pulled up on the right side, as if he was always about to smile. But Principal Montgomery very rarely smiled at anything and he was feared by all the pupils – and staff – for his severity on any matter of discipline.

As usual, he was wearing a tiny plastic flower in the lapel of his hounds-tooth check sports jacket. Before carrying on he flicked a switch on his intercom. 'No interruptions, please, Miss Stubbs.' Jimmy heard the electronic chirping of the reply.

'Bad business, Marvin.'

'Yes, Sir.'

'A bad, bad business. Yes, I can say without fear of

66

contradiction that this is a bad, bad business we have here.'

It didn't seem like any kind of answer was required, so the boy sat still and quiet. All around him he could sense the humming heart of the school. A class was chanting poetry and somewhere he could faintly hear the tinkling of a piano. Stopping and then beginning again.

'I have in front of me, on this piece of paper, a list of everyone who has spoken to me about this sorry affair. Do you know how many names there are upon this list, Marvin?'

Jimmy thought that was a bit of a silly question. How could he know? 'No, Sir. I don't know how many names there are.'

Montgomery nodded solemnly. 'Quite right, son. You don't. But I know. And I'm goin' to tell you how many.'

But for several stretched seconds the Principal said nothing. Peering down at the typed list as though it might somehow hold the secret of the universe. In the background the music stopped, made a false start and then stopped yet again.

'Mr Eatham is at the head. I have spoken to him on seven separate occasions. Miss Stubbs entered them in my diary for me. You know your father has been to see our English visitor in my presence?'

'Yes, Sir.'

It had been the day after Eatham's ill-mannered interruption of the football training session. Dad had taken an hour off from the busy restaurant and gone up to Porchester. When he returned he'd slammed the front door of the Victorian-frame house so hard that the glass had rattled in every window. He'd then walked straight out of the back door of the house to cool off in the woods around, not returning for nearly three hours. Jimmy never heard the details, but it obviously hadn't been a very successful or friendly discussion.

'It was not a happy meeting, Marvin,' continued Principal Montgomery. 'I was forced to intervene to prevent fisticuffs. Happily, I was in time. However, when Miss O'Keefe asked for a similar meeting with Mr Eatham, I regret I was too slow to stop an ugly scene ensuing. Miss Stubbs aided me in separating them as they rolled around on this carpet. On this very carpet.'

Jimmy glanced down, hoping to see some blood-stains. There'd been rumours of a fight, but no proof. 'Who won, Sir?'

The Principal's mind had wandered away. 'What? Oh, I'm happy that Miss O'Keefe upheld the honour of Thomas Melville by bloodying his nose and . . .' He recollected who he was talking to. 'That's no business of yours, Marvin.'

'No, Sir.'

'Miss Deurson threatened to resign over this bad, bad business.'

'Honest?'

'Altogether there have been well over a dozen requests by members of staff to try and persuade me to over-rule Mr Eatham. I have had my supper interrupted by phone calls from members of the Parent-Teacher Association. Even the Mayor himself has been in touch. It would mean a lot to Porchester to win Halloween Bowl.'

'You think this makes me feel any better, Sir?' said Jimmy. 'I know all this.'

'You see, son, I'm stuck in between a rock and a hard place. You may be telling the truth and then again. . . . Well, I even called up Mystic Seaport and spoke to the man who jumped in and saved young Eric. He was nearest and he said he couldn't rightly be sure. But he thought it was the grown-up who stumbled and pushed the kids. That's what he said. But I fear that Mr Eatham is immovable.'

'And wrong.'

Principal Montgomery stood up, moved away from his desk and looked out of the window. 'Snow on the way,' he said. 'Your class have this fall hike next Wednesday, don't you? With Mr Eatham again, I believe.'

'Yes, Sir. Supposed to be on a walk around Mount Cardigan.'

'Hope he takes more care, what with the ice and . . . but let that pass.'

'Is that all, Sir? Only, I'm not sure why you wanted to see me. Nothing changes, does it? Nothing can change, either. Why d'you send for me, huh?'

The Principal moved to stand by the boy, placed his hand on his shoulder and spoke very quietly. 'I'm not sure, either, Jimmy. I guess I just wanted you to know how sorry . . . how very sorry I am about this whole damned business.'

* * *

The Fall Ramble was an established part of the semester at Thomas Melville Junior High. During the last week of October, before the bad weather finally began to close in on New England, the top year would all go out to different locations for a day's hiking. And Jimmy's class had indeed once again been landed with the hugely unpopular Englishman.

On the Saturday morning, Jimmy was sent by his father on an errand to Uncle Frank's house. To deliver a note about the coming month's finances for The Olde Roaste Beefe. Bookings were getting busier and busier and Burge was suggesting to his brother that they should think about taking someone else on for the lunch-time trade.

It was a crisp, sunny morning, and Jimmy jogged halfway across North Strafford. Keeping himself in trim ready for next week and the big . . .

'No point,' he said to nobody in particular. 'No point bothering.'

Coach O'Keefe had called round the previous evening and left a photostat copy of the playbook. She urged him to keep in training and make sure he knew all the moves of the squad. Mum had asked the tall woman why there was any point?

'Could be Mr Eatham still might change his mind at the last minute. He's under some real heavy press-ure in the staff-room, Mrs Marvin. Or, looking on the bright side, he might fall under a bus or catch leprosy.'

The two women laughed together, but Jimmy could tell how fed-up Miss O'Keefe was. To get to the Halloween Bowl and then lose her star player.

'At least Eric's all right,' he said.

'Yeah, Jimmy. But the engine's only goin' to be firing on half its cylinders. Still, I gotta go. Remember that Starship song a coupla years back. It's not over till it's over, Jimmy. So keep fit.'

He remembered that and started jogging again, pumping his arms for extra effort. Whistling the song to himself. Letting the beat of the music coincide with the beat of his trainers on the blacktop.

'It's not over, till it's over.'

Eddy opened the front door. 'Hi, Jimmy. Heard about that guy barring you from the Bowl. Real tough luck, man.'

Jimmy sighed. 'One of those things. I'm right and yet I'm the one gets pushed down the tube. Is your father in?'

'Sure. In the kitchen eating breakfast. Go on through.'

Jimmy walked into the living-room, which was in semi-darkness with the curtains drawn across the windows. He could hear his aunt and uncle talking beyond the next door. As he picked his way round the end of the large, saggy sofa, he nearly tripped over something on the floor.

'Aaaarrgh . . .' he gasped, stumbling sideways.

'Watch where you're goin', you clumsy . . .'

Now his eyes were becoming accustomed to the cavernous gloom, he saw what it was. Saw *who* it was.

'Sorry, Angie.'

'That you, Jimmy?'

'Yeah. Just passing on through.'

71

He bent over to stare more closely at his cousin. Since she'd started her modelling course Angelina Marvin had begun to behave kind of oddly. But this was really something else.

She lay on the carpet with her bare feet raised on a couple of house bricks. She was wrapped in a sheet that looked as though it was wet. But what took Jimmy's fascinated gaze was his cousin's face. It looked like one of the top quality side salads that they served in their restaurant. Several thin slices of cucumber covered Angie's eyes. Wafers of avocado were laid in strips down her cheeks. All over her forehead and down either side of her nose was a sticky mush that looked, and smelled, like it was made from a purée of raspberries and strawberries. Her mouth peeked out from behind a mound of shredded lettuce leaves, some of which had spilled down on the floor.

'You still there?' she mumbled.

'No. I'm gone.'

Uncle Frank was perched on a stool at what they called their 'dinette', tucking into a plate of scrambled eggs with some strips of crispy bacon. He raised his coffee cup to Jimmy. 'Hi. Fancy a mug of Laura's best java?'

'Yes please. Quite cold out.'

'Sure is,' said his skinny, elegant aunt, pouring him a cup of steaming coffee. 'Eddy let you in?'

'Yeah. Saw Angie on the way through the living-room.'

Frank laughed, stroking his enormous walrus moustache that drooped down both sides of his mouth. 'Boy, this modelling by mail is gettin' out of hand.

72

I've heard of a girl lookin' good enough to eat, but I never thought my own little girl would literally look like a fruit and salad mix.'

Like everyone else, the American half of the Marvin family had heard all about Jimmy's troubles at the Junior High.

But Laura was more interested in an item of gossip that she'd picked up down at the village store the previous day.

'Is it true your sister's gotten herself engaged, Jimmy?'

'Kate and Deke Koslow?'

'That's what they say, honey.'

Jimmy grinned. 'I don't know. I guess Kate sees a lot of Deke. They're out together most evenings and weekends. I suppose it wouldn't be all that surprising if they got engaged.'

'But you got more important things on your mind, Jimmy?' said Uncle Frank. 'Heard about it from Eddy and from your Mom an' Dad. Whole of Porchester's talkin' about it.'

'Really? That just makes me feel worse, you know. Like I keep saying, it's not as if I've done anything bad. I told the truth and I'm the one getting punished for it. Not fair.'

'Local Chamber of Commerce have been on the line to Doc Montgomery, your Principal. He just says his hands are tied by "professional etiquette". Guess that means he can't call that English . . .' Uncle Frank checked himself from saying anything too strong. 'That English teacher the liar he really is.'

★ ★ ★

When Jimmy got home again, he found that Chris had locked himself away in his bedroom. In the last three weeks he'd started looking smarter when he went to the High School and finally admitted: 'There's this girl, bro.'

Now 'this girl' had materialised. A tall, solemn first year who was already in the school's basketball squad. Her name was Caroline Haddad and she lived in an isolated house deep in the forest between North Strafford and Porchester. 'Her father', Chris said proudly, 'was a draft resistor during the Vietnam War and was on the run from the authorities.' Jimmy had been surprised to learn that the woods around Vermont and New Hampshire had been thickly dotted with young men who'd fled the military call-up in the late sixties and early seventies.

Kate was out with Deke, visiting his parents for lunch.

The weekends were specially busy times at the restaurant. They were booked up for Sunday brunches for about two months ahead and Saturdays were nearly as crowded. Dad was already down there, putting the finishing touches to the noon special. Today it was smoked salmon flown in exclusively from Scotland, served with buttered potatoes and cress.

Jimmy wandered down into the kitchen of their home, and found his mother sitting at the big scrubbed pine table. She was surrounded by dozens of pieces of paper, marked 'Invoice' or 'Statement'. Mum had her pocket calculator in front of her. She didn't even look up when her youngest son walked in.

'Hi, Mum. Anything I can do to help?'

'Yes. Push off.'

'Oh.'

She sighed and put down the calculator. Half-smiling at him. 'Sorry, love. I'm just swamped in trying to get these figures to make sense for the Internal Revenue Service. What we used to call "income tax".'

'Could I do anything?'

'Not really. It's the price we pay for the restaurant being so successful. Mustn't grumble. Tell you what, Jimmy.'

'What?'

'You could bring in some logs for the stove. Getting cold these afternoons.'

'That's Chris's job this week, Mum,' he protested. 'I do it next week.'

'All right, but you offered to help. Don't if you can't be bothered.'

'No. That's not. . . . All right.'

'Thanks, love. I'll be done with all this figures and stuff in about an hour. I'll make lunch then. How 'bout a nice omelette?'

'Can I cook something for myself? I'd like to do a pepper and tomato sauce with some spaggers.'

'You had spaghetti yesterday, didn't you? Oh, never mind. Yes, do that for yourself.' As he was about to go to the larder Mum called him back. 'And do us a portion as well, please.'

In the afternoon Jimmy went and sat alone on his bed. He picked up the list of offensive plays that Coach

O'Keefe had left for him. But after a few moments he dropped it on the floor. There wasn't any point.

Despite all of her attempted encouragement for him.

It *was* over.

 It was the idea of Bobby Sheldon's older brother, Keith.

'It's great, Jim,' said Bobby. 'It'll discredit the Rotter and it'll take all the heat off of you and it'll mean you can play in the Halloween Bowl on Saturday and . . .'

'Hang about, man. Hang about.'

The usual group of friends were gathered together at recess on Monday. In their usual corner of the Junior High's playground, between the Science Block and the Main Hall. It was a bright October morning, with a few scattered clouds scudding high across the bright blue bowl of the sky. As they talked, their breath came feathering out in the cold air.

'Tell us, Bobby,' said Hunter Goldblum. 'Any idea's better'n no idea.'

'Yeah. I guess so,' agreed Jimmy Marvin, slouched disconsolately against the red-brick wall behind him, hands in pockets.

'You're gonna be a downer then forget it, man,' said Bobby. 'I mean . . .'

Declan McMurdo punched Jimmy on the shoulder. 'Loosen up, Jim. Give it a try.'

'Sorry. Just that I don't see much light at the end

77

of the railroad tunnel. Unless it's a train coming at me.'

'We get a surprise witness. Like those old Chief Ironside adventures on television. The guy in the wheelchair who wins all his cases. There's always a surprise witness. And we got one.'

'Who?'

Bobby Sheldon grinned round the circle of friends. 'Ethel Murgatroyd.'

'Who?'

'She's an old widow who lives up near Mystic and she happened to be there that day and she saw the whole thing and she's got a nephew lives around Porchester and he told her the news and so she's gonna write to Doc Montgomery and tell him how it was.'

By the end of that sentence Bobby had run out of breath and turned red in the face with the effort.

Jimmy couldn't believe it. For a few moments none of the group spoke. Each of them savouring the wonder of the news. A witness who'd support Jimmy and who'd denounce Mr Eatham. Everything was suddenly going to be fine.

'What d'you think, guys?'

They all looked at Jimmy. 'I think . . . I can't believe it, Bobby. Can't believe it's true.'

There was a cackle of laughter. 'Course not, Jimbo. That's 'cos it's *not* true.'

'What? How d'you mean?'

'I mean that Ethel Murgatroyd is really gonna be my good old brother. Keith'll motor to Mystic to post the letter. That way ole Doc won't suspect a thing, will he?'

Eric Wood put on his best Bugs Bunny impersonation. 'Errr, what's up Doc?'

Everyone except Jimmy Marvin fell about laughing, slapping each other on the back. Until they noticed that he wasn't looking too happy.

'Errr, what's up, Jimmy?' said Eric.

'I really. . . . I mean, it's nice that your brother tried to think. . . . Look, guys, there's no way it'll work.'

'Why not?' said Bobby Sheldon, indignantly. 'It'll clear everything.'

'You reckon Doc Montgomery's a fool? No, seriously. Course he's not. He plays everything by the book. Sure he'd like to believe that kind of mystery witness. But what's the first thing he'll do when he gets this letter?'

'How d'you mean?' said Bret Dillon, puzzled.

'I mean that he'll want to call up this Ethel Murgatroyd, won't he? Just to check out the details before he shows the letter to Eatham?'

The noise of the other boys and girls enjoying their morning break seemed to swell as the group of friends fell suddenly silent. Bret Dillon spoke first.

'He'd try and call her up.'

'We could say in the letter she didn't have a phone,' tried Bobby.

'He'd write. Before he did anything, he'd check it out, wouldn't he?' said Jimmy, pressing for an answer.

'Might not,' Bobby said, defensively.

'Some hope,' Hunter said. 'Nice try, man, but

Jimmy's right. Doc Montgomery might be a mean mother, but he's not stupid.'

The bell rang, signalling the end of the recess, and they filed slowly and disconsolately back into their classrooms.

There were just five days to go before Halloween Bowl.

Almost from the dreadful moment on the football training field when he'd broken the news about the ban, Mr Eatham had been consistently pleasant towards Jimmy. Almost as though he felt that he'd won a final, crushing victory and could afford to be magnanimous to the defeated.

But his classes were still brimming with tension. There wasn't a single boy or girl at Thomas Melville who liked the tall Englishman. There'd been some wild talk about a strike and everyone refusing to go to Eatham's classes. But Miss Deurson had moved among the children, counselling caution. Pointing out that it could do no good for Jimmy and his cause, and would probably alienate the Englishman still further.

But it didn't stop them from reducing their classroom cooperation to the absolute minimum.

Whenever he asked a question, not a single hand went up. Jokes were met blank-faced and silent. Homework was done to the lowest possible standard.

He had, however, made one effort to win them over, on the previous Friday, towards the end of their double lesson with him.

'Class,' he'd said, clapping his hands. 'Come on kiddies. Pens down a moment. I just want you girls and chaps to know that I didn't want to ban our James there from this big match.'

'Then why d'you do it?' asked a chubby girl, Wilonia Tyas, who sat right next to Jimmy.

'Like John Wayne said, my dear, there are times that a fellow must do what a fellow has to do. I hoped that the American sense of fair play would have appreciated that. Obviously I was incorrect.'

'Obviously,' whispered someone from near the window.

Mr Eatham's face grew pale, apart from the two scarlet patches across his cheek-bones. His lips tightened and his eyes almost disappeared. 'Very well. Pick up your pens and carry on writing.'

Wednesday morning came around. The day of the Mount Cardigan hike. Jimmy and his training friends would normally have been looking forward to the day off school. During their time around the dome-topped mountain they'd jogged or walked most of the wood-land trails. If it hadn't been for the presence of Anthony Charles Eatham, it could have been a relaxing day to cherish. Just seventy-two hours before the tension of the Halloween Bowl.

But now it was just another dreary day to drag through. With the braying voice of the English teacher like a hacksaw down the edge of a sheet of plate glass. A constant reminder to Jimmy of his miserable plight.

When they gathered together in the car-park of the Junior High, waiting for the coaches, there was a general atmosphere of gloom. All the boys and girls were wearing either hiking trainers or walking boots, with lightweight back-packs. All of them had brought sandwiches and plenty of fruit juice to drink. Jimmy's father had given him a large thermos of hot beef and vegetable broth.

Mr Eatham turned up looking a poem in designer pastels. Pale blue waterproof trousers tucked into a brand new, squeaky-clean pair of pale green hiking-boots. A light blue sweater with a matching anorak over the top of it. His rucksack still had its new label dangling from the back.

'Looks like he's ready for the High Sierras,' whispered Bret Dillon, starting into a fit of giggles amongst the boys around him.

'I've heard of the king of the wild frontier, but that's ridiculous,' said Hunter.

'He sure looks loaded for bear,' sniggered Wilonia.

Jimmy didn't join in the laughter at the teacher's expense. He felt oddly detached from it all. He just wanted the day to be over so he could get home and go up to his room, shut the door and put on his ear-phones. Turn the 'Motown Hits Of Gold' up to nine on the volume control and let it wash him away.

Principal Montgomery had come out to see the top year off. Standing on the school steps he made a short speech to them all.

'The Fall Hike is here once more. My goodness, but how that old clock does roll around. Another year gone. The year dying away and winter waiting in the wings with snow on its breath.'

'He's a poet, an' he knows it,' said Jeremiah Carson. Despite his handicap, the teenager wasn't going to be

82

left off the walk. Jimmy knew that he had already completed a twenty-five mile hike for charity. He also knew that Mr Eatham had tried to have Jeremiah taken off the Mount Cardigan trip, on the basis of not wishing to look after someone who was disabled.

'I have checked with the weather bureau and also called Mount Washington for a forecast update.'

Jimmy knew about Mount Washington. The whole Marvin family had gone up there by car on a quiet, calm summer afternoon. But by the time they reached the top they'd found a howling gale blowing. Uncle Frank had told them that Mount Washington was literally the windiest place on earth.

'The late morning will be clear with temperatures rising into the low twenties Celsius. Not more than a five per cent chance of any precipitation. Staying mainly fine in the afternoon. But there is a note of caution which I want you all to heed.'

'I'm heeding, I'm heeding,' hissed Andy Poscotis, getting the expected laughter from his friends.

'I am advised that temperatures will plummet, yes, postively plummet, once the sun has dipped. So if you are on the shadow side of the mountain you can look for the hazards of ice. Therefore, exercise the greatest care. Now you all have a good day and all return here safely by four-fifteen this afternoon.'

Mr Eatham sat in solitary splendour in the double seat immediately behind the driver. Apart from several warnings about noise from the back of the coach, the teacher said nothing to anybody.

And nobody spoke to him.

9

As they were alighting from the coach at the foot of the mountain, Anthony Eatham caught at Jimmy's sleeve.

'One moment.'

'What?'

The teacher led him a few yards away from the rest of the class. Dropping his voice so that nobody could overhear them.

'If you could see your way clear to admitting that you were wrong . . . or that you *might* have made a mistake, Jimmy, then I might be able to see my way clear to remitting the punishment.'

'I lie and I play. Is that it . . . Sir?'

Eatham had pasted a smile on his mouth, but it was in grave danger of slipping away. 'Perhaps you were mistaken, Jimmy. It happens. But I have my reputation. I am an Old Etonian, you know?'

'That mean you went to Eton?'

'Indeed. And there is a matter of honour, you see.'

Jimmy shook his head. 'I want to play in the Halloween Bowl more'n pretty well anything in the wide world. But not enough to tell a lie for it. Sorry, Sir. Looks like I get to keep my honour and you get to keep yours, doesn't it?'

'Very well,' hissed the teacher. 'I have given you your chance and you have rejected it. There will be no more chances.'

Eatham was flourishing a huge map, trying to unfold it in the strong breeze that was blowing in from the north. The children stood around in twos and threes, waiting for the signal to get moving.

An elderly couple, dressed in well-worn hiking clothes, came down off the trail, pausing as they caught sight of the English teacher in his new-minted outfit.

The old man was right by Jimmy and his friends and he cackled with laughter. 'Hey, guys! Old teach there looks real pretty, don't he? All ready for a fashion show.'

Eatham must have heard the comment, but he studiously ignored it, turning his back and peering intently at his map.

'He takin' you up yonder in them clothes? Hope he don't get no dirt or nothin' on 'em. Spoil the nice colours!'

His wife pushed him with a bony elbow in the ribs. 'Leave him alone, Edgar. Let the kids go hikin' any way they want.'

'When you comin' back, mister?' the man asked Anthony Eatham.

'Are you addressing me?'

'Well, there's only you an' me and I ain't gone so far that I talk to meself.'

'Yes. We plan our return close to four, o'clock this

afternoon.' Adding sarcastically: 'If that meets with your approval?'

The old man tugged at the lobe of his left ear, glancing at the sky. 'Ain't a question of my approval, mister. Just that any guy takes a bunch of wet-nose kids up Mount Cardigan, this time of year, ought to be darned sure he knows what he's doing.' He sniffed and turned away, throwing over his shoulder: 'Darned sure.'

Hunter asked whether the group of friends who knew the mountain so well from their training sessions could move on ahead of the main party and meet up at the top. But Mr Eatham pointed out that he was in charge of the hike, that he had prepared carefully, using the map and a guide-book, and he would be leading the party.

'Me and only me. I am the leader. I've done a lot of hiking in England, you know. Offa's Dyke. Hadrian's Wall. South Downs Way. I think you'll find that I'm pretty experienced, sonny.'

The lower stages of the walk were easy enough. Winding around the flank of the hillside, picking their way through the fallen leaves. Most of the fiery colours of autumn had gone and the trees were mainly stark and bare. The sun shone bravely down and even amongst the woods it still felt fairly warm.

Streams ran ceaselessly over stones dappled with emerald moss. The play of sunlight over the dull brown earth cast dancing shadows all around the feet of the children.

There was nobody else out walking on Mount Cardigan that late October morning. Mr Eatham led the way, despoiling the calm freshness with a braying commentary as he went.

Not all of it that accurate.

'Keep close together, children. No straggling. I want to stop for lunch quite soon. But watch out for snakes. And remember that this is bear country. See a grizzly and you run like blazes. They won't follow you.'

'No grizzlies round New England,' said one of the girls in the party. 'My Aunt Carla's a Ranger in the National Parks and she says that if you meet a grizzly in the back country you move off slow and easy and keep out of its way.'

'I'm jolly certain I could outrun a bear, Alice,' said Eatham.

But the girl wasn't about to be sidetracked. 'No, you couldn't, Sir. They can run faster up hills or down hills or on the flat. And they can swim faster as well. Young grizzlies can climb trees real well, too, Sir. But there aren't none here, so don't worry.'

'I am not worried. Thank you for the nature lesson, Alice.'

'Real welcome, Sir,' she replied, ignoring the sarcasm.

A little later Jimmy felt one of the laces snap on his trainers.

'Oh . . . shoot!' he exclaimed. 'Bret. Ask the Rotter if he can stop and wait for me while I fix my sneakers, will you?'

'Sorry, laddy,' was the reply from the teacher. 'Should have checked out your equipment before we started. Good workman doesn't blame his tools, Jimmy. Time waits for no man. And neither do I. Either catch us up or you can go back down to where the bus'll be coming later.'

'We're stopping for food soon,' said Declan. 'Can't really lose us on this trail. Not in this weather. You'll catch up real quick, man.'

Jimmy wasn't honestly in any hurry to catch up with the rest of his class. So much of the conversation had been about the prospects for the big match in three days' time. The strengths and weaknesses of the Castle Rock Junior High. It wasn't that any of his friends tried to keep Jimmy out of the conversations. But he still felt isolated and excluded. Everyone kept returning to his barring from the Bowl. 'Yeah, but if only Jimmy hadn't . . .' and then stopping, the sentences trailing away.

The noise of the group disappeared surprisingly quickly amongst the trees. The boy sat there, the sounds of the woodland returning all around him. The rising wind in the naked branches and the tinkling of the streams.

It was a relief to be able to sit down on a large frost-cracked boulder and listen to the soothing noise of the flowing water. He unthreaded the broken ends of the lace and knotted the frayed parts together. Carefully relaced it, working his way up from the toe-end of the trainer. His head bent over the task, his tongue pushed between his teeth in concentration.

Conscious of something moving at the corner of his

vision, he looked up. A pair of squirrels had come down from a nearby tree and were scavenging amongst the leaf-mould, barely a dozen feet away from him.

The boy didn't move, fascinated by the darting speed of the little creatures. Time drifted by and he had no sense of its passing. Nature surrounded him and for a few minutes Jimmy was contented.

It was a magical moment and he treasured it. The closeness of the squirrels and his complete isolation from every other living soul. He never told anyone, ever, about the shimmering peace of that moment.

His footwear repaired, Jimmy jogged easily up the winding track, finding that the party had stopped just around the flank of the mountain, at a point where several trails intersected.

'I'm delighted that you've consented to honour us with your presence, Jimmy,' greeted Anthony Charles Eatham.

He didn't reply. There wasn't any point. Everyone was scattered around the clearing, busily opening packs of sandwiches, peeling off layers of foil, and tearing at waxed containers of soft drinks and fruit juices. Jimmy picked his way over legs and rucksacks, and joined his usual group of mates. Hunter shuffled sideways to give him room to sit down.

'What kind of food you got?' asked Bret, eyeing Jimmy's pack greedily.

Jeremiah Carson unpeeled his food. Groaning loudly. 'No. Oh, no. Not cheese and tomato. I hate cheese and tomato!'

'How come your Mom made you something you hate?' asked Hunter.

Jeremiah grinned. 'She didn't, man. I made 'em myself. But I sure hate cheese and tomato sandwiches!'

The group all laughed at Jeremiah's loony sense of humour.

Jimmy uncorked the thermos and poured himself a mug of the steaming soup. It smelled delicious and tasted even better. In the box there were a couple of crusty wholewheat rolls with some honey-glazed ham and slivers of fresh pineapple, with cottage cheese on top. His friends all watched him at his lunch with envious eyes.

'Boy,' said Declan. 'I sure wish my old man could do great food like that.'

There was a chorus of agreement from all the others around him.

The break became longer and longer. Hunter, watching the teacher carefully, said that he thought that Rotter was having problems with his smart new hiking boots. Saying he reckoned that was why they'd stopped early for a meal and why there seemed no hurry in getting moving again.

'Well past noon,' said Jimmy. 'If'n we don't get a move on soon then we'll never reach the top before the sun goes down the far side. Goin' to get real cold then.'

'Mebbe you should go and tell your buddy from the white cliffs of Dover to hurry up and get us all hiking?' suggested David Locke, the football team's kick return specialist.

'Yeah. Or maybe I ought to just go and jump in the stream? And you with me,' grinned Jimmy.

Time passed.

Looking up the rounded face of the mountain, it was possible to see that the reddening globe of the sun was already scraping close to the summit.

As Jimmy stood up and stretched he noticed that he could now see his breath in the cold air. He'd saved about half of the flask of soup and he wondered whether he'd finish it off. Deciding it might be better to keep it for later.

'We goin' to the top, Sir?' asked one of the girls in the class.

'Of course. Suppose we ought to be toddling along now. Come on, everyone. Don't dawdle around. Up and going.'

He conveniently ignored the fact that everyone else had been ready for over half an hour.

There was a direct trail to the top of the mountain. From their training runs, Jimmy knew that it was wide and simple, without any obstacles or sharp turns. Using it, they could be at the summit in well under an hour.

'We'll go this way,' said Eatham, commandingly. Pointing to the meandering track that wound around the side of the hill, towards an area that Jimmy and his friends knew was furrowed with deep ravines and gulleys.

Hunter put his hand up, calling out hesitantly. 'Quickest way's up there, Sir.'

'Too steep. Map shows this as easier. Got to think of the young ladies in the party, don't we?'

Bret Dillon stood by the skinny boy. 'He's right, Sir. Some of us know Mount Cardigan real well. The direct path's heaps better.'

'Don't argue with me. Wastes time, boy. I have my map.'

Jimmy opened his mouth to join the protests, then closed it again, recognising the futility of it. Eric Wood tried instead.

'Side trail's rough. Take us hour to an hour an' a half to the top that way. By then it'll be freezin' and the track down could be tough.'

Eatham actually stamped his foot. 'I will not have this disobedience! I am in charge. Another word and the football team will be missing several more of its allegedly important members for Saturday's game. Follow me!'

The sullen crocodile of teenagers filed along the narrow, winding trail, following the pastel colours of their teacher's hiking clothes. Within forty minutes the sun had already begun to tip below the summit and the temperature was dropping fast.

The sky had clouded over and on two separate occasions there was a flurry of rain that glistened on the rocks and trees. Just as Jimmy and his friends had known, the path became narrow and indistinct, eroded in parts, with a sharp fall to the left.

The children began to slip and stumble.

Which simply provoked anger from Anthony Eatham at their head.

'For goodness sake! Can't you be more careful? I do believe you're just doing this to antagonise me. Look where you're going!'

Jeremiah Carson was finding it hard going and Jimmy and Bret had moved forward together to lend a hand when it was needed.

'Not far from the top now!' carolled the English teacher, who was now limping badly on his right foot, often wincing and trying to ease his new boots.

'Sun's full gone now,' muttered Hunter Goldblum. 'I tell you, I don't like this, guys. If he keeps on up we're gonna get stuck there for the night. I can see it happenin' to us.'

'Barrel of laughs, Hunter,' said Wilonia Tyas. 'Any of you got any spare food? I ate all mine and I'm gettin' kinda hungry.'

'Any food anyone's got, they better keep it,' warned Jeremiah. 'Hunter's right. This is getting way, way beyond a joke.'

'I didn't think it was ever very funny,' commented Jimmy.

'Stop the chatter at the back!' shouted Mr Eatham.

Eric Wood suddenly slipped, saving himself by putting a hand down onto a boulder that glistened like glass. 'Hey!' he exclaimed. 'It's ice. Not water, guys. It's sheet ice.'

Immediately, everyone was reaching out, touching the stones, the trees, the wet earth. All of them finding the same. A delicate tracery of lethal ice was forming across the mountain.

Jimmy touched the bole of a birch tree. It looked as though the drizzle had simply left a film of water on

93

the trunk. But the tips of his fingers told him the real story. Slick ice coated the trunk – and the branches and the twigs and the dark, delicate leaves.

'Gordon Bennett!' he said, unconsciously using an exclamation of his gran's. 'That's amazing. It's formed so quick.'

'What's going on down there?' called Eatham. Pausing at an angle of the trail, where it hung over the lip of a drop to some scrubby bushes and stunted trees. Up to his right there rose the bare stone of the final hundred feet or so of the mountain's summit.

'It's icing up!' shouted Hunter. 'We have to go back.'

'Have to? We *have* to, do we, Goldblum? Are we the teacher then, are we, Goldblum? We're in charge all of a sudden, are we?'

'It's darned dangerous, you . . .' began Jeremiah Carson.

'Maybe for someone with your problems, son. Not for . . .'

Slightly off-balance, his boots slipped on a patch of puddled ice. And Eatham vanished over the brink of the drop.

Oddly enough, he didn't cry out as he was falling. The loudest sound in the sudden stillness was the brittle snap of a bone breaking.

Only then did Anthony Eatham begin to yell.

 Jimmy Marvin could never quite work out why it was that it had been him that took charge of the situation on the frozen slopes of Mount Cardigan.

Even when he looked back on the afternoon, there still didn't seem any clear explanation for his assuming leadership of the party.

Mr Eatham had disappeared over the brink of a steep drop, rolling and clattering through the brush. There'd been the dry-branch sound of a bone breaking and then the yelling.

And Jimmy had spoken: 'Hunter. Bret. Declan. Come down with me. Gotta get him back up on the path. Rest of you just shut up and don't all mill around. You're like a load of headless penguins. Keep quiet!!'

The commanding voice of the English boy rose above the hubbub. But down below, the teacher's cries for help still soared over everything. Jimmy picked his way cautiously to the icy edge of the trail and peered down. With the sun already well out of sight, the light was fading fast and he could barely make out the sprawled figure of Rotter, on his back, moaning quite piteously.

95

'Keep still, Sir. Some of us'll come down and bring you up here. Then we can decide what to do.'

'Well get a bloody move on, boy. I've broken my damned leg. Hurry up!!'

Jimmy called his friends around him, issuing his orders, which nobody even tried to contradict. Behind them, Mr Eatham was still mumbling in a mixture of shock and pain. But they'd carried him up and Jeremiah, who'd done a first aid course, had rigged up a makeshift splint with a couple of broken branches and some straps from rucksacks. The Englishman had kept complaining about how uncomfortable the splint and his leg were.

'Don't worry about it, Sir,' grinned Jeremiah. 'You'll find out you can get used to it.'

Jimmy glanced around the circle of friends. 'Listen. Be dark quite soon. Can't move him on our own. Main thing is to get as many as possible to the carpark.'

Hunter nodded. 'Take time, though. Can't rush with everything frozen now.'

'And someone has to stay with him,' said Eric, gesturing with his thumb at the teacher.

'One of us has to go and get help. Stretcher and all that. Means someone's got to try and make it to the bus. There's an emergency phone down there.'

'Who?' asked Wilonia.

'Me,' said Jimmy, without a moment's hesitation. 'I'm fittest. Pretty well fastest. I know the mountain. And if I get hurt . . . well, it won't kind of harm the team for Saturday's game.'

96

One by one his friends agreed with him. Hunter Goldblum summed it up. 'Can't argue with you on any of those points.'

'Right,' said Jimmy. 'Hunter and Eric gotta lead the rest down. You know the trails. Take it easy and slow. But you'll still be down before it gets to be fully dark.'

'How about the Rotter?' said Jeremiah. 'I'll stay with him. I can come down with the rescue party.'

'I'll stay as well,' offered Declan.

Bret Dillon punched the air. 'Me too! Yeah, me too.'

'I'd like to stay,' said Wilonia Tyas.

'Sure. Four's a good number. I'll leave the flask. Still some hot soup in it.'

Jeremiah Carson took it. 'Good. Main thing we have to do is try and keep Eatham warm. He's gone into shock and he'll start hypothermia. Anyone spare a jumper or an anorak?'

Jimmy shrugged his way out of his coat. 'Good thinking, man. Take mine. It'll only slow me on the run down.'

Altogether they managed to scrounge enough surplus clothing to almost bury the teacher. At least he wasn't going to freeze. The four children who were to stay with him had also borrowed extra layers for themselves. Even if things went well, it would be at least two hours before help arrived.

Anthony Charles Eatham was looking deadly pale. His lips were grey and he was trembling. Jimmy and the others explained what they were going to do and the teacher insisted on trying to shake the boy's hand.

'God bless you, Jimmy. God bless you. Be as quick as you can, dear boy.'

Hunter and Eric walked with Jimmy a few yards towards the main trail intersection.

'Watch it, man,' urged Hunter. 'Ice is real, real bad. Sure you know the way?'

'Course. Still a bit of light. I'll bring them here before you know it.'

It was a blur of nightmare speed.

The cold bit at him as he started the precipitous descent of Mount Cardigan. Once he'd run for three or four minutes he began to warm up, but his breath enveloped him. Tendrils of mist appeared near the dozens of streams that honeycombed the surface of the hill. Once a deer leaped from the gloom, as startled by the boy as the boy was by the animal.

The sun was fully gone and the first evening stars were beginning to sparkle like the diamonds on a jeweller's black velvet cloth. The trail was coated with ice and Jimmy's feet slipped again and again. But his balance as a running back served him well. He jinked and dodged around trees, just like he did on the football field. Just like he had, eighteen months earlier, in the streets of South London. But this time there wasn't time for any fantasies about playing in a big game.

This was for real, and the teenager's concentration was total.

He lost count of the number of times that he actually fell. But most times he just slithered on his bottom for a few yards. A couple of times he went down more heavily, rolling in a kind of judo break-fall.

His instinctive sense of direction kept him moving along the right paths, always downwards, towards the car-park.

Before he realised it, there were the lights of the school bus, waiting for him, its engine throbbing quietly in the stillness of dusk. The driver was sitting behind the wheel, doors and windows all closed against the frost, eating an iced doughnut and reading the sports pages of the local newspaper.

Jimmy was aware, all at once, of how near the ragged edge of exhaustion he was. There was a cramp under the ribs. His chest hurt and the breath was rasping in his throat. His leg muscles were all protesting against the dangerous run and there were cuts and grazes on both hands from his tumbles.

Jimmy banged furiously on the doors, until the driver lazily threw the lever that opened them.

'What's the. . . . Boy, you're in a heck of a mess, son!'

'Accident. Teacher broke leg. Phone rescue. Need stretcher.'

The driver dropped his newspaper and jumped to help Jimmy to a seat at the front of the coach. 'What about the rest of the kids? They still up on the mountain, there?'

Jimmy shook his head, still struggling for breath. 'No. Coming down slow and careful with guides. Four stayed with teacher. Very icy up near the top.'

'That guy must be a damned fool, leaving it this

late to try and get off the hill. Will you be able to lead them back to find him, son?'

'Yeah. Can you go and phone?'

The driver left him in the bus and ran to the emergency telephone. The rescue party arrived just about the same time that the rest of the children eventually, and safely, picked their way down the trail into the car-park.

The men were equipped for all kinds of rescue, with floodlights, ropes, a doctor, dogs and a stretcher. Their leader was a bearded man in his early forties who came and spoke to Jimmy immediately on their arrival.

'You ran down Mount Cardigan, son?'

'Had to take a couple of chances. I know the trails pretty good.'

'You did real well. I'll make out a report after this is over and I'll say that. You're English, aren't you?'

'Sort of. Lived here a year-and-a-half. We're going to become citizens, my mother, brother and sister and me.'

The man nodded solemnly. 'Let's get to it. Can you find them again?'

'Definitely. Even in the dark.'

'You're not too tired? Don't answer without think-ing, Jimmy. This isn't a macho game. You fall behind then we all fall behind.'

'No. I see that but I reckon I'm all right. Shall we go?'

'Sure. The driver'll take the rest of your class to

their school and messages will be given to the folks of the kids still here.'

To his embarrassment, the boys and girls gave Jimmy three rousing cheers before they were driven away into the darkness.

The lights carried by the rescue party threw the hillside into startling relief. Trees became etched black and water ran silver down the narrow valleys. The ice was everywhere. Jimmy had been given an extra-thick anorak to keep him warm as they all trudged up the trail.

'Must be a good ten below,' said one of the men, hunching his shoulders against the wind.

On the side of the path, Jimmy noticed a strange and beautiful creation of nature.

Water trapped in small twigs had begun to freeze. As it expanded it was forced out through tiny holes in the bark, like miniature fountains. The air was becoming so cold that those almost invisible sprays had frozen, in the most wonderfully delicate filigree shapes.

'Call 'em "fairy crystals", folks do,' said one of the men, shining his light on some of them. 'Real pretty, ain't they? Touch 'em and they just crumble in your fingers.'

Mr Eatham was looking pretty sick by the time they eventually reached him and got him strapped on to a stretcher. The leader of the rescue party didn't seem that worried about his condition. 'Shock is all. Considering how long he's been up here, and the weather, you kids have all done marvellously well. Whoever splinted him made a real neat job. How d'you keep him warm? This flask?'

'Soup my Dad made,' said Jimmy, proudly. The four friends who'd stayed up the mountain with the injured man all grinned at each other. Sharing the enormous relief that it was all over.

And it was all fine.

'And your Principal, Doctor Montgomery, has given your whole class the day off school? Is that right, Jimmy?'

The boy nodded nervously. This interview, for local television, was infinitely worse than the dark run down the ice-slick trail of Mount Cardigan.

'I've heard the story from your friends and from other teachers how you and . . .' pausing while he consulted his notes. 'Mr Eastham were . . .'

'Eatham,' interrupted Jimmy.

'I'm sorry.' Calling to the director behind the camera. 'Can we just cut it there, Helen?' Back to the boy. 'You mean I got his name wrong?'

'Yeah. Eatham. Eat, as in tuck into food and ham as in bacon. Eatham. Get it?'

'Got it. Right, Helen. Can we do it again?'

The long-haired girl behind the camera motioned for Mum and Dad Marvin and Chris and Kate to keep quiet. 'Running. Sound. Go.'

'I've heard the story from your friends and from other teachers how you and Mr Eatham were not exactly the best of friends. And that he banned you, the Thomas Melville star running back, from the Halloween Bowl on Saturday.'

'That's true,' said Jimmy.

The interviewer smirked knowingly at the camera. 'Now you did that heroic run to save his life, you figure that teacher might change his mind, Jimmy? Huh? What d'you guess?'

For a moment the boy didn't answer. But his mother did. From the corner of their living-room she said, very audibly: 'If he doesn't, then he's even more of a creep than I thought.'

'Cut,' said the director, wearily. 'Please, Mrs Marvin! Can we try it one more time?'

Miss Deurson met Jimmy at the door to the classroom before Friday morning's registration. 'Doctor Montgomery wants a word straight away,' she said.

'About tomorrow's game?'

She shrugged. 'I don't know. I hope so, but . . . you know his feelings of loyalty towards staff? Anyway, he doesn't always take me into his confidence. Just hurry along.'

'Yes, Ma'am.'

'And, Jimmy?'

'Ma'am?'

'We're all very, very proud of what you did on Mount Cardigan.'

'Thank you, Ma'am.'

Miss Stubbs giggled as Jimmy walked into the outer office. Known affectionately as 'Chubby Stubby' by all the students at Thomas Melville Junior High, she waved the boy through.

'In you go, dear,' she said. 'I was so pleased to see you on television last night. And so proud of you.'

'Thanks, Miss Stubbs.'

He knocked and entered, finding Doctor Montgomery standing by the window, gazing out at the rolling New England hills. He turned as Jimmy entered.

'Come in, my boy. Come in. Sit down. Good. Well, this has turned out a pleasant business, has it not? Indeed it has. A shame for poor Mr Eatham, of course, but a great credit to our beloved school in the way you all rose to the occasion.'

'Thanks,' said Jimmy, shuffling his feet nervously on the carpet.

'Now, I have some very good news for you, Jimmy. Very good news.'

This was it! The boy suddenly felt light-headed with relief and excitement. Eatham had taken back all his lies about the incident at Mystic Seaport. Everything was going to be fine. The Halloween Bowl would be the great conclusion to his last gridiron season at Junior High. Immediately his mind went to some of the key plays that he'd be involved in during tomorrow afternoon's game.

But the Principal, smiling broadly, was still speaking.

'I had a call last night at my home, just after we'd finished dining. I recall that my dear lady wife had done her special of baked cod in the most delicious sauce with. . . . But that is by the by. Let it pass. The call was from the head of the Porchester Chamber of

Commerce who had watched you on the seven o'clock newscast.'

He paused, and Jimmy realised that some kind of comment was needed. 'Yeah, Sir?'

'Indeed. And I would have to say that he was in the very best of spirits. There was a monthly dinner for the Chamber last night and they held a small collection for you children.'

'Really, Sir?' said Jimmy. Wondering when the Principal was going to get a move on and reach the bit about Halloween Bowl.

'Really. Now, let me consult my notes to make sure that I have all the facts at the tips of my fingers. Yes. Here we are. They have given ten dollar tokens to both Hunter Goldblum and Eric Wood for their efforts in leading the remainder of the class safely down Mount Cardigan.'

'That's nice of 'em.'

'Indeed it is. The token may be encashed at the book-store here in Porchester. Twenty dollar tokens for Jeremiah Carson, Wilonia Tyas, Declan McMurdo and for . . . who was the fourth child that remained behind with . . .'

'Bret Dillon, Sir.'

Principal Montgomery beamed at him, stroking down the straggling ends of the ginger moustache. 'Very good, my boy. Bret Dillon. Yes. Each gets a twenty dollar gift token.'

This was all interesting to Jimmy, but his mind still remained hooked to the news about Halloween Bowl. When was Doc Montgomery going to finally get around to that news?

'But for you, James Marvin. . . . The Porchester Chamber of Commerce has authorised me to inform you that as a reward for your courageous initiative in the most hazardous circumstances, you are to receive a token for one hundred dollars. It will be given to you at a public presentation next week by the Mayor of Porchester herself. Well? You don't seem very pleased by all this, Jimmy?'

'I'm sorry, Sir,' said Jimmy, puzzled. 'Course I'm pleased about the . . . but is that all?'

'All?'

'Yeah. I mean. You haven't said anything 'bout tomorrow?'

'Tomorrow, Jimmy? I'm afraid that I don't quite understand what . . .'

'The Halloween Bowl, Sir.' The boy was becoming desperate. How could the head of the school not know what he meant?

'I'm aware that it is. . . . Ah! *Now* I begin to perceive what. . . . You came here hoping that I would tell you that you could play for us tomorrow. Oh, my dear young man. I am so sorry.'

'You mean I'm still . . . still not playin'! I don't believe it.'

'Please don't cry, Jimmy. You must try to realise my position.'

'Your position?' shouted Jimmy angrily. 'And I'm not cryin'. I'm just. . . . That creep tells lies, then nearly gets us all killed and you still . . . You still can't see that . . .?'

The Principal stood up from behind his desk. 'Jimmy, Jimmy.' Miss Stubbs, hearing the noise, stuck her head around the door of the office. She retreated when she caught the Principal's angry glare. 'You must not talk like this.'

'Why not?'

'Mr Eatham, as I have explained to you before, young man, is a member of my staff. Whether I believe him or you is not the point I must confront. I must support my teachers or there would be anarchy. Plain and simple anarchy. If Mr Eatham were to leave then things would be very, very different. I assure you of that, Jimmy.'

'Fat lot of good that is to me an' the team and the whole rotten school!'

Jimmy stood up and made for the door, Doctor Montgomery following him. 'What about the hundred dollars, Jimmy?'

The boy paused. 'Tell 'em to stuff their hundred dollars, Sir. I won't touch it!' And he went out, slamming the door behind him.

 The Marvins sat together in the third row of the grandstand. During the previous evening, Jimmy had told his parents that he didn't think he really wanted to go along to the Halloween Bowl. But they'd talked to him about it, pointing out that all his friends on the team would be disappointed if he wasn't there to watch and cheer them.

'To enjoy anything, you have to involve yourself in it,' said Dad.

Chris sat on one side of Jimmy, with Eddy on the other side, delving into a huge box of popcorn. Kate and her boyfriend, Deke, were next along, with Aunt Laura and Uncle Frank at the end of the row. On the row immediately in front there was Dad with Angie. The girl was wearing tight stone-washed jeans and a ragged top, her eyes hidden behind an enormous pair of designer sunglasses, which Laura kept telling everyone had cost more than all the rest of the outfit put together.

Mum wasn't there.

Jimmy was aware that some kind of mystery was being played out between his parents, but he couldn't work out what it was. At first his mother had been the

108

most keen of all to come and watch the match. Then, after a late-night phone call, she simply said something had turned up. But if all went well she'd be along around half-time.

'Do you actually know where she's gone, bro?' Jimmy asked.

Chris shook his head. 'No. But I saw her checking out the route down to Boston. Guess it's something to do with the restaurant.' He stood up and looked around. 'Can't see Caroline anywhere. Boy, she's always late.'

'There she is. Behind the marching band.'

Chris's girlfriend waved as she saw the Marvins, picking her way along the crowded rows of seats to join them.

The sportsfield was an amazing sight. Every seat was taken and spectators lined both sidelines. It had been a struggle for Dad to keep a space for Mum to join them later. Rather a big space, Jimmy noticed, for just one person.

With its motif of Halloween, lots of people had turned up in appropriate costumes. Witches and magicians abounded as well as lots of Jimmy's friends in a variety of pumpkin attire.

Now that he was there, Jimmy somehow didn't feel quite so bad at missing the game. At least Mr Eatham wasn't there to complete the ruin. The boy had been down on the field as the two teams started their pre-match warm up, wishing everyone luck, shaking hands and patting shoulders.

All he could do now was sit back and cheer his loudest.

The brass band was playing a strange Academy Awards version of Michael Jackson's 'Thriller'. On their side of the field, the Thomas Melville mascot was whipping up the crowd's enthusiasm. The mascot was a plump little boy from the seventh grade with a huge, grinning pumpkin on his head and a black cloak spangled with stars and moons and he was leaping insanely along the front of the grandstand.

'We're gonna rock Castle Rock!' he kept on yelling in a shrill, breaking voice.

Jimmy dug his hand into the proffered container of salted and buttered popcorn, sitting back and enjoying the beautiful autumnal sunshine. The band was playing its way through all the hits of Michael Jackson. At least, that's more or less what it sounded like.

But the music suddenly faltered, brass screeching, drums losing the beat.

'What on earth?' exclaimed Dad.

'Look,' said Angelina, half-standing. 'Who is that amazingly grodey person?'

'Grodey' was the trendy word of the week amongst Angie and her mall-pack friends.

The whole crowd watched in stunned amazement as a figure came bursting through the marching band, throwing them into a chaotic confusion, the music faltering away into dissonance. There was a great nodding pumpkin head of orange plastic, set on top of a coat of garbage bags and black tights. And feet encased in bright red slippers shaped like tomatoes.

The head turned from side to side as it scanned the crowd, seeking someone. To Jimmy's horror, and embarrassment, the creature seemed to be seeking
110

him. The arm pointed to him and the muffled voice sounded like it could be calling his name.

'It wants you, son,' said his father.

The hands were clawing at the plastic dome that shrouded the head. The person was desperately trying to say something, but nobody could understand it.

Finally, the head was torn away, revealing the scarlet, sweating face of Doctor Montgomery, eyes open wide, gasping for breath.

'Jimmy Marvin! Just had a call from Logan International Airport in Boston. From Eatham. He's quit and flown home to England. He's not on the staff here anymore.'

'Then . . . ?' said Jimmy.

'Course. Said so, didn't I? Get changed, lad. You're playing!'

 Coach Christine O'Keefe did everything she could while staying the right side of the rules to delay the start of the game. Giving her star running back as much time as possible to race into the locker-room and start getting himself kitted up. Jeremiah Carson had hobbled along after Jimmy, helping him get taped and dressed, adjusting the shoulder-pads and handing him the Number 26 helmet.

'Good luck, man,' he said.

'Thanks, mate. I'll need it. Not warmed up and I haven't had time to kind of build up any concentration. You know?'

'Yeah. Go, Jimmy!'

As he ran on to the field, pulling his jersey down over his shoulders, Jimmy heard a roar from the Porchester fans. Out of the corner of his eye he glimpsed Miss Deurson, wearing a lopsided witch's hat, waving to him.

Castle Rock had kicked off, resplendent in their white and royal blue gear. Thomas Melville were in their usual scarlet and gold strip.

David Locke returned the kick out to his own twenty yard line, where he was drilled by one of the

112

opposition covering players. Jimmy ran straight into the huddle, grinning round at all his mates, getting welcoming grins in reply.

The play was called and, as they broke up, Jimmy pulled on his helmet, buttoning the strap around his chin. It was a straightforward start, typical of the beginning of any game, with offense and defense testing each other out.

Jimmy's role was to block the opposing outside linebacker. The count was completed and the ball snapped into the hands of Eric Wood. But Jimmy didn't find the power he expected and the Castle Rock boy shrugged him off.

Declan had just taken the ball on the called play when he got hit and knocked back for a net loss of two yards. It was a bad start and Jimmy's failure to check the defense knocked some of the heart out of the Porchester team. Eric threw two incomplete passes on the next two downs.

While the kicking unit took the field, Coach O'Keefe didn't spare Jimmy in her scathing comments.

'Call that blockin', kid? Because I sure don't. You wanna play, Jimmy, then show me. If you don't then you can go sit on the bench for the rest of the afternoon. Understand?'

'Yeah, Coach. You know that I can play when . . . I just got to get warmed up. Get my mental attitude right as well.'

She shook her head. 'I don't know, son. Maybe this is all a big mistake.'

★ ★ ★

The next few minutes were a nervous interchange with the defenses on top. Castle Rock had a chance with a forty yard field goal but the ball just dipped under the cross-bar.

Jimmy took off twice in the next series, but each time he was nailed at the line of scrimmage and knocked down without a single yard's gain. Fortunately for the Porchester team, their passing game was beginning to click. Eric hit Hunter and then Bret with long passes on successive downs to carry them up to a first and goal situation on the Castle Rock five yard line.

Jimmy was finally shaking off the lethargy and shock over his last-moment selection. On first down he managed to get outside, around the corner, running the sweep to the one yard line. It took two linebackers and the strong safety to drive him out of bounds.

Second down and a fake pass to Jimmy. But the defense weren't fooled and picked up the actual pass to Declan, knocking him down for a net loss of three yards.

Third and four. Jimmy went for the dive over the top but one of the Castle Rock defenders just caught him by the ankles and held him at the one yard line.

Coach O'Keefe sent in the signal telling them to go for it. Fourth and one. The possible touchdown was balanced by what would have been a certain field goal.

The Castle Rock coach knew that Jimmy Marvin was the big threat on a short yardage call and he gambled on the ball going to him.

He was right.

Jimmy took the hand-off from Eric and powered

straight up the middle. Virtually the whole eight defenders hit him. He went down fighting, but he went down short.

Coach O'Keefe patted him on the back as he came off, head down, disappointed. 'Lookin' better, son. You'll get there next time. Nice try.'

The Porchester defense did their stuff and forced Castle Rock to punt from deep inside their own half. Their kicker was an enormously fat boy with a lethal right boot.

Jimmy went on punt return, feeling the concentration flowing back, the energy seeping into his muscles. It was a towering kick, hanging in the cool, sunny afternoon air, spiralling end over end. Jimmy positioned himself under it, keeping his mind clear of the rushing opponents, taking the ball into his hands. A large boy in white and blue was on top of him, but Jimmy spun away from him, shrugging off two more ineffectual tackles. A gap appeared on his right and he pushed off a defender and headed for it.

'Put him away!' screamed the Castle Rock coach, from the nearby line.

With a rush of excitement Jimmy saw the path was clear to the end zone, with only the punter waddling hopelessly across towards him.

The tracks of the two boys intercepted right on the five yard line. It was so easy that Jimmy never even bothered to try and dodge around his clumsy opponent, content to use his own speed and impetus to go clean over the boy.

Instead of lowering his head and hoping to miraculously stop the running back, the punter stood his ground and slapped out at the ball, tucked casually . . . too casually . . . under Jimmy's right arm. The Porchester boy was so surprised that he tripped and rolled into the end zone, not exactly knowing what had happened. Just aware that he was over the line but he no longer had the ball. Jimmy rolled up on his knees and looked behind him, seeing the chubby punter clutching the ball, going down valiantly under a wave of scarlet and gold.

Shaking his head ruefully, Jimmy trotted over and helped the punter scramble to his feet. Nothing was spoken as the two boys grinned at each other. But the expression on the fat kicker's face said it all. 'Hey! I don't believe it either.'

Jimmy smiled and shook his hand. Though the moment had gone against him, that was what the game was all about.

Porchester's defense played well, but the visitors managed to nickel and dime their way upfield on a series of short passes and tight running plays. On the ten yard line the quarterback fooled everyone with a fake hand-off, spearing in a short touchdown pass to his unmarked tight end. The kick after was good and the scoreboard clicked to seven to nothing for Castle Rock.

At the beginning of the second quarter, Porchester were rocked on their heels by a series of great offensive plays by their opponents. Two very long passes connected and the home team was suddenly staring at a twenty-one to zero whitewash.

Coach O'Keefe tried to rally her squad, but they

were shell-shocked. She took Jimmy on one side, bending over him to talk quietly and insistently. 'Heart's slipping away. Heads comin' down. You're the best on the team, Jimmy. Best I ever coached. If you're ever goin' to show folks your class, it's now. Go for it, son.'

First time he got the ball in his hand, he set off like a runaway artic lorry, exploding into tacklers and always struggling for that extra yard, in the spirit of the greatest of them all, Walter 'Sweetness' Payton.

The drive carried Thomas Melville Junior High right down to their opponents' line. It was a third and two play and Christine O'Keefe sent in the signal for Jimmy to try and run it in, on a wide sweep around the end.

The ball was snapped and Jimmy took it, clutching it tightly to avoid another fumble. He ran hard, parallel to the line, looking for a gap to appear. The other Porchester players threw themselves into blocking.

The gap was there! And Jimmy dived for it, head down. A scant yard short. Then the Castle Rock middle linebacker appeared, as though he'd been fired from a circus cannon, going helmet to helmet with Jimmy. Who wasn't prepared for the violence of the hit.

His head snapped back and as he blacked out he felt the ball slip from his grasp. His last thought was a bitter regret that he'd lost it yet again.

Short seconds later he regained his senses and the first thing he saw was Hunter Goldblum leaping around in the end zone, waving the ball over his head.

Jimmy decided that he was probably dreaming and slithered off again into the darkness.

'How many fingers am I holdin' up, kid?'

'Butter, I guess, Dad.'

'What?'

'I said . . .' His eyes opened and began to focus. He saw the team doctor looming over him, like a far-off face seen through a peephole.

Fortunately, half-time was only a couple of minutes away and Porchester turned around with the score at twenty-one to seven. And Jimmy had time to recover from the blow. Apart from a bit of a headache he didn't feel too bad. He lay down resting, while Coach O'Keefe gave them a pep talk.

Gran came and spoke to him. 'If you beat this lot I'll buy you an ice-cream, son.'

Then he knew he was still dreaming. Blinking his eyes open and seeing his mother and grandmother standing together.

'How did . . . ? I mean, is that you, Gran?'

'Course it's me. Who d'you bleedin' expect? Cilla Black? That'd be a surprise, wouldn't it?'

'But you're . . .' Realisation dawned. 'That's where you went, Mum. Boston Airport.'

His mother smiled. 'Right. I've heard about what happened. Never guess who I saw hobbling towards the Departure Lounge?'

'The Rotter?'

'Got it in one. Can't say he looked too happy.'

'Serve him right,' sneered Gran. 'Nasty little . . . !'

'Careful, Mum,' warned Jimmy's mother. 'Language.'

'Well. . . . He was. Now you get stuck in, son, and treat us to a win. Score some goals, or whatever it is you score.'

By the start of the third quarter, Jimmy was really pumped up. The Porchester defense forced a fumble early on and they took the ball over on their opponents' twenty-two. The teenager thought of all the people who'd canvassed so hard to get him into the team and he knew in his heart that he wasn't going to disappoint them.

On the first down Eric Wood pitched him a short pass and he was off and running. Dodging the linebacker and rocking the safety on his heels. Suddenly he was into the Castle Rock secondary and sprinting down the field, cutting inside the desperate tackle of the corner back and high-stepping into the end zone.

It was a great start to the half.

But the rest of the third quarter continued the unremitting battle, with the defenses holding the balance of power. Two field goal attempts by Porchester were thwarted by a great block and a fumbled snap. The fourth quarter began with the score frozen at twenty-one to fourteen to Castle Rock.

With nine minutes remaining, quarterback Eric Wood generalled a great drive up the field, beginning way back at their own five yard line. With Jimmy blocking and running his heart out, the scarlet and gold advanced towards the opponents' end zone.

It ate up five minutes off the clock, but it brought

them finally to the Castle Rock sixteen yard line, where the momentum faded in two incomplete passes. Third and ten.

The defense read the call as a pass to Jimmy, arrow-straight up the middle. They fought their way towards the small figure, seeming to engulf him. The home crowd' cheering hushed away, suddenly bursting into a deafening crescendo. Jimmy had stayed on his feet, twisting like an eel, emerging from the tangle of bodies with the ball in his hand. A stutter step around the last man and he was in for his second touchdown.

Eric and Hunter led the rush and it seemed as though he'd been buried under the whole squad. Helmets rattled exultantly against his, grinning faces under every mask.

The kick after sailed high between the posts and the game was tied up at twenty-one each.

Four minutes and six seconds remained.

The Porchester defense, spurred on by the hoarse yelling of Coach O'Keefe, put in a last stupendous effort. Pinning Castle Rock back. But the visitors weren't down and out yet. They pulled out a series of big passes, as they had in the first half, coming perilously close to a touchdown.

But the last, vital pass was a finger-tip interception, giving Thomas Melville the ball.

One minute and fifty-eight seconds on the clock.

The coach didn't panic, sticking with Jimmy – knowing he was the best card left in her hand. And he didn't disappoint her. One minute and twenty-two seconds later he'd pushed and swerved and dodged and battled for her and for the team. Driving himself to the brink of exhaustion and beyond it. Taking them all the way up the field to the enemy nineteen yard line.

Christine, seeing how tired her favourite player was, called a time out. Beckoning both Jimmy and Eric Wood to her side.

'Well, guys? They'll look for a last drive from Jimmy and then the field goal. We aren't goin' to give 'em that. We're goin' to win in style.'

Jimmy grinned. 'I know, Coach. It's time for Three L Way Right.'

She nodded. 'You got it, boy. This'll bring 'em out of their seats. Go for it.'

Eric took the call into the huddle. Jimmy remembered that they'd been trying it out at the moment that Anthony Charles Eatham had dropped his bombshell on them. Was that a bad omen or a good one?

The ball came into the hands of the slim, black quarterback, who slipped it to Jimmy. The receivers all dashed into the end zone and were promptly covered. The rest of the defense watched Jimmy as he feinted left, and then cut back right.

Nobody watched Eric Wood.

He strolled unmarked into the end zone, suddenly lifting an arm to give Jimmy the target. Nobody was within ten yards of him.

Jimmy had been keeping an eye on him, watching the rushing defense. The tall nose tackle had broken through and was in his face but he remained calm, cocking his arm and floating the pass to the waiting quarterback.

Hunter and Bret picked up the only defenders who

might have menaced the pass, and the ball reached Eric's hands. Jimmy dodged the Castle Rock player and watched, thinking he'd never seen anything quite as beautiful as the sight of the black teenager running into the end zone, ball held triumphantly over his head.

'Touchdown!'

The whole of the Thomas Melville squad piled on top of Eric, but Jimmy held back. He knew what it was like to lose a big match and feel the pain of the winners' jubilation. Knew how it hurt. Instead he started to shake hands with the opposition, giving them praise. Telling them to stay healthy. Their day would come. Maybe next year at full High School level.

It was a class performance.

An hour or so later, after all the locker-room celebrations and a tearful speech from Coach O'Keefe, Jimmy walked out to rejoin his family. Mum had gone with Kate and Uncle Frank's family. Dad was helping Gran to their car.

The boy found himself alone on the partly-lit field, silent and deserted after the afternoon of high triumph. The turf seemed to vibrate under his feet with the energy of the game.

Jimmy suddenly thought of the young boys, like himself, who'd played on this cropped grass, for decades before him. The ground had so much history, and Jimmy Marvin felt proud to be a small part of it.

His older brother's hand on his shoulder drew him from his thoughts. The boys stood quietly together for a magical few seconds, neither speaking. Not needing to speak in the shared moment.

Finally, Chris broke the night silence: 'Come on, bro,' he said. 'It's time to go home.'